SEEDS OF WAR

BOOK 2

Scorched Earth

A Semper Fi Press Book

Edited by Elektra Hammond and with input by James Caplan and Kelly O'Donnell.

Cover by Jesh Snow

DEDICATION

To the SMOFs and fans who created

the San Juan, Puerto Rico NASFiC
and the Helsinki, Finland WorldCon.

Your tireless efforts produced many wonderful
outcomes, including two authors from different
worlds coming together in the unlikely partnership
that resulted in this book.

Thank you.

Seeds of War
Book II: Scorched Earth

Part I: Any Landing You Can Walk Away From

You never forget your first taste of combat. That first low orbit insertion where you plunge from the belly of a spacecraft and plummet like a fireball, your battlesuit ready to take on any opposition. Every mission is different, as is every world—the feel of the gravity, the taste of the air—but the planet of your first fight with the enemy gets imprinted on your brain, good or bad. For Lieutenant General Colby Merritt Edson, Republic Marine Corps (Retired), that world had been New Mars, more than fifty years ago.

It had also been the site of his greatest failure, a battle of politics and misplaced trust. He'd tried to do what was right for the Corps, tracking down and ferreting out the bastards sending substandard equipment and ordnance to the men and women who were risking their lives

1

for the Republic, only to be screwed over by politicians and corporate ladder climbers eager to make money without regard for the damage they did along the way. But those bastards enjoyed the wealth they had skimmed, and they had power. Colby had been willing to risk his career for the good of the Corps, but in the end they had won by threatening his people. He could walk away or watch as they destroyed the lives of men and women like Jonas Venango and Li Siniang Greensboro, whose only crime was being extraordinary Marines. For their sake Colby accepted "voluntary retirement."

To avoid unfavorable optics they'd pushed him through one of the many wormholes on the elliptic above New Mars and dropped him on Vasquez, a nearly empty agricultural world. He had a farm, an agcomputer that did all the work, an old dog, and a kit full of recriminations and regrets.

And now he was heading back again, albeit not in any fashion anyone could have ever imagined. Alien plant soldiers had destroyed almost everything and everyone on Vasquez. As proof, Colby had hotwired the boss alien's ship for his ride.

The absurdity of sitting on the deck of an alien vessel felt oddly calming after the last couple of days of fighting plants. He absent-mindedly rubbed Duke's head as the ship continued its climb into the space surrounding Vasquez. His command-grade implant had managed to connect with what was a one-level vegetable control system. It wasn't a perfect interface, though; there were many blank areas his implant could not interpret. Colby had been able to take off from the planet's surface, however, as that was nothing more than feeding the engines power and pointing it in the right general direction. Trying to make it through the wormhole and then back to New Mars would not be so easy. A slight miscalculation, a slight gap in the ability to work the controls, and instead of easing smoothly over the event horizon of transition, he and Duke could nick the perimeter of the wormhole and be rendered nothing more than pink mush by tidal forces beyond the explanation of physics.

Assuming that didn't happen, they'd either get there or they wouldn't; there was no chance of ending up somewhere else. Vasquez's star system was no different from eighty percent of systems with wormholes, which is to say it only had one. Fly a vessel into it without bouncing off the edge and you came out the other end, sometimes hundreds of light years away. Sol system was one of those which filled most of the remaining twenty percent by boasting two different wormholes, one on the ecliptic above the orbit of path of the asteroid belt—and there was no shortage of boffins and squints who thought one had a lot to do with the other—and one further out above the Kuiper Belt.

But a fraction of a percent of star systems had more than two wormholes. Ninety-eight percent of these had between three and six, providing not just gateways between worlds, but interstellar highway interchanges. And the remaining two percent of that original fraction had stupid numbers of wormholes. No one knew why. There was no pattern. It didn't seem to relate to the type of star, the number or kind of planets (if any), moons or not, or anything else. It was just the luck of the draw. To date, the Republic had identified seventeen star systems with an excess of ten wormholes each. The system containing New Mars had thirty-three, the fourth most of any of them, and all of them clustered in the ecliptic above the one planet. It wasn't an interstellar highway, it was a freaking hub of endless high-volume traffic with well-regulated guidelines and time tables for what could come through which wormhole when, which despite a fleet of AIs still saw the occasional collision at speeds where even a small nudge or graze was deadly, and none of the objects coming through any of the holes in space were anywhere near small.

He would be arriving above New Mars without benefit of the schedule for when something was expected to emerge from the Vasquez system transit. Space is vast, but the sheer amount of traffic—both manned and automated—coming and going above New Mars made it seem snug. There was a very real chance that he would collide with something before the traffic control AIs could do anything to stop it. It didn't matter how fast their dedicated brains could calculate, some things just came down to mass, velocity, and distance.

Colby chose not to think about that.

The ship didn't have anything that looked like seats, so he sat on the deck, back up against the rubbery bulkhead. Duke was lying beside him, head on his lap as he petted her. She was calm, happy to be with him. She wasn't thinking about the wormhole. She didn't have the imagination to picture what could happen, what could go horribly wrong.

No, I'm not going to think of that. Think of happy thoughts, Edson, like just being alive.

Most of the people on the planet had evidently been killed during the plant invasion. For all he knew, Topeka was the last human left on the planet—well, she and Riordan, stuck in his med chamber. Staying behind as she had done was probably the smart thing to do. Eventually, someone would come to find out what happened, why the agricultural shipments had ceased.

Colby didn't have that luxury. He had to report back to the government reps on New Mars so they could get word back to Earth. He had to prove to Vice-Minister Greenstein and the rest that there was a threat out here in the far reaches of human space, that aliens had arrived at Vasquez without benefit of any wormhole. Which in turn suggested technology beyond anything humanity possessed. And if aliens had stumbled upon Vasquez, then how long before they noticed the wormhole to New Mars and its cornucopia of routes to dozens of other human-inhabited worlds? Fifty years before, Colby had helped wrest control of the system from a fringe government, back when they'd only discovered five wormholes there. He'd damned well do all he could to ensure aliens didn't get their hands on it now. Before lifting off from Vasquez, he'd downloaded a complete account of the plant invasion and sent that forward. He couldn't be sure it'd be read, or if anyone would believe him.

In a way, he couldn't blame them. It was pretty fantastic. A sentient plant had invaded Vasquez with millions of plant minions that had destroyed everything in their path. He wouldn't have believed it if he hadn't seen it with his own eyes.

"How about you, Duke? Would you have believed it?"

Her eyes remained closed, but her tail gave a weak thump on the deck.

He looked around the ship. It was somewhat sparse, but with the help of his implant, he'd worked out which mossy patches and which knobs and roots were actually instrumentation, enough to let him know he was inside a ship. Instead of control seats with harnesses, there were ropy, vine-like arms that were pressed against the bulkheads. Several had been connected to the king plant when he and Topeka had entered the bridge, but they had released it once the fight commenced. These tendrils still slowly reached out, as if wanting to embrace him. Colby wasn't up with that, which was why he'd settled on the deck just out of their reach.

With dampeners that were not as effective as in human ships, the gentle shifts in pressure were evidence enough that they were in motion. He contemplated querying his implant to find out how long before they entered the wormhole, but after a moment, he decided against it. Better to be like Duke and remain blissfully in the dark.

He couldn't just sit there, though. He gently slid Duke's head off his lap, then stood up, looking around the bridge. He wandered over to the so-called instrument panels and tried to make some sense of the displays, noting the vines and keeping away from the leafy ends.

"What's this?" he asked his implant, touching one of them at random.

"That displays the atmospheric content inside the ship."

When he'd first followed Topeka and her machete-wielding charge into the ship, he'd worried whether the atmosphere was even breathable. After taking his first breath, he'd forgotten about it. Now, his curiosity was piqued.

"What is the oxygen level in here?" he asked.

"O2 level is 17.9 percent."

That was a little light for most terraformed worlds, but well within human tolerance. Some of the Phase 2 worlds, already inhabited, had far lower percentages while the terraforming process continued.

He was about to ask what other traces were in the ship's atmosphere, but he realized he didn't care. He was breathing. Duke was breathing. That was enough. He asked because he was trying to keep his mind off of the wormhole.

Nope, I'm not going to think about that.

He turned away from the displays, ran his hand across the bulkheads, and wondered as to their structure. They weren't metal or any of the substances used in human ships, but they didn't quite feel organic. They were clearly made from some sort of vegetative matter.

Maybe a plant alloy? Is that even possible?

Whatever it was, it would keep the scientists busy for years—if he got it back in one piece. If he didn't wreck the thing by clipping the edge of the wormhole or smashing into other traffic once he reached the other side.

For God's sake, Edson! Get your mind off of it. You've faced death before, so put on your big boy pants!

And he had faced death—more than once. This time, though, was different. He didn't have much control over what was happening. He could fly the ship, but not well. He was essentially a piece of cargo, an unexpected shipment that wasn't on anyone's schedule.

It was what it was.

One of the vines reached his boot, and he spun around and strode to the back of the bridge in search of another distraction. He pressed the side of the slit along the bulkhead. Nothing happened. He raised his hand higher, pressed again, and was rewarded when the slit opened up to a small cold storage locker. There, trussed up on the deck, was the headless body of the dead plant-thing, with its head jammed between the body and the bulkhead at the back of the locker. Inside, several vines had emerged to encase the body, but he thought it was a little late for whatever they could do for it.

"Sorry," he said, poking the body with his finger. "But maybe you'd prefer this than to be a lab sample."

He'd wanted to keep the thing alive, and he'd had it restrained when Topeka, angry at losing her co-worker Sestus, had taken the thing's head off with her machete. If that was its head, that is. For all he knew, its brain was deep inside the torso. One thing was for sure, though—it was stone-cold dead.

Colby didn't know how long it would take to navigate the alien ship. He was gambling that once he emerged from the Vasquez wormhole, an AI traffic controller would send a cargo drone to tow him safely planetside. He wanted to make sure the alien didn't decompose like the plant soldiers had on Vasquez, so he had his implant query the ship's control system. There wasn't anything that could act as a morgue on board, but the locker/alcove/whatever in the back could be kept at a cooler temperature. That had to be better than nothing, and even if the thing did decompose, whatever was left would be easier for the science-types to scrape out.

It had taken a good five minutes to horse the thing into the locker. Its limp, dead weight had not been easy to handle. But he managed to stuff it in, Duke looking on in frank confusion as he did so.

With a sigh, he touched the other side of the opening, this time hitting it correctly, and the locker closed.

Now what?

He hadn't explored the rest of the ship yet. The bridge took up at least a third of the ship's length, but that meant there was still two-thirds that he could explore. He doubted that he could learn much, but it was better than just sitting around with his thumb up his ass.

"You coming?" he asked Duke.

She opened her eyes, wagging her tail twice, before she got up and padded over to him. He reached down and petted her head.

"Yeah, who's a good girl, huh?"

A ripple passed through Colby's body, as if his insides were trying to become his outsides and then back again.

Duke shook herself once, twice.

"Did we pass through the wormhole?" he queried his implant, standing up and looking around as if he expected the ship to be coming apart.

"Affirmative."

"And, are we. . . are we OK?"

"Wormhole insertion accomplished within standard parameters."

"Well, hell, girl. That wasn't bad at all," he told Duke, who wagged her tail in response. "A little more topsy-turvy than usual, but what the heck, right?"

Duke thumped her tail. Good enough. But they wouldn't remain in the wormhole for long. Time inside was relativistic. Some claimed it lasted days, others just seconds. After what seemed only a minute another ripple ran through the ship. They were back in normal space.

"And. . . uh, where are we?"

Colby had the coordinate inputs to get back to New Mars, courtesy of Topeka, but that didn't mean they'd entered the wormhole at the slender window to arrive at a known location.

"We are within the RS402 funnel."

Colby gave a sigh of relief. Every wormhole had an active outer rim where piloted vessels emerged and a narrower, inner funnel used by automated cargo pods and similar craft.

"Are we within range of a cargo drone?"

"Affirmative. I have activated the transponder, and it is aligning for an intercept."

Getting through the wormhole to the RS402 funnel had been the hard part. Between his own implant and the transponder codes that Topeka had provided he anticipated no difficulty in getting the funnel's designated AI to assign a cargo drone to react and capture it. They were still a long ways from the planet, and by surrendering control to the drone Colby wouldn't have to rely on his limited skill with piloting the alien ship in order to get there on his own. If the drone could grab the alien ship, then it would carry them to New Mars without any more action on his part.

He wandered back to the control panel. Surely there had to be some form of video display.

"Can you show me the cargo drone?" he asked.

"Affirmative. It is on the display now."

Colby didn't see anything that looked like a view of space, and certainly, he couldn't see a drone.

"I can't see anything."

"The feedback circuits indicate that it is being displayed."

Colby could swear that his implant sounded a little peeved—but that was impossible, right?

"Upload a visual."

Colby gave the mental command, then blinked three times, taking a biological snapshot that his implant could analyze. Controlling his beta waves like that was beyond most people, and most implants didn't have the capability, but he'd had years of practice, so it was almost second nature to him.

"The feed is not visible," his implant told him.

No shit.

"As I said. I guess the interface isn't perfect. But, you're sure the drone is on its way to us?"

"Affirmative. ETA in eight minutes, forty-two seconds."

Unless your interface is screwing up.

Colby chose to assume the drone was approaching. If it wasn't, he'd figure out how to navigate the plant ship to New Mars under its own power.

"Well, Duke, we'll just see what happens now, huh, girl?" he said, patting her on the head again.

She leaned into his leg and wagged her tail, forehead pressed up against his hand. He was suddenly struck by how much she trusted him. He'd never had a pet while on active duty, and he'd taken care of her at the farm more out of responsibility than anything else. Yet here she was, on an alien ship, trusting him to keep her safe.

And he was glad she was with him.

"Give me a countdown on the drone's arrival," he said, still petting Duke.

"Five minutes, twelve seconds."

He took a seat, out of reach of the vines, and Duke snuggled her head in his lap. Unlike the last time he was sitting, he was now totally relaxed. What could go wrong now? It was nice to be able to simply sit back, petting his dog. As soon as he landed, he'd have to jump into action, forcing Greenstein and the command to understand the threat. Hostile first contact, right on the doorstep of one of humanity's most critical systems. Assuming they believed him.

It's going to be hard for them to ignore this ship, though, and the dead broccoli man in the locker.

"Four minutes," his implant told him as he closed his eyes.

He'd been up and running almost since the plant soldiers had attacked his farm. He didn't know how long it would take the drone to get him to New Mars, didn't know where the RS402 funnel was in relation to the planet in its orbit. Surely there'd be time to get some shut-eye once they were on their way.

"One minute."

Heck, that seemed like five seconds.

He knew he'd fallen asleep, so he opened his eyes, slid a protesting Duke off his lap, then stood up.

"Plenty of time to sleep as soon as we've been grabbed, girl."

He waited for confirmation, his nerves stepping up a bit. There were thousands of the drones around New Mars at any given time handling the many shipments coming in from dozens of wormholes. Transponder codes indicated which were to be sent down to the planet's surface to one of many depots for handling and processing, and which had to be rerouted on to one of the many other wormholes for the next stage of their journeys across space. A hundred AI traffic controllers routed ships from ingress to egress with rarely an exception that had business down on New Mars itself.

A jolt well beyond the capacity of the ship's dampeners staggered Colby and knocked Duke off her feet.

What the hell?

Most of the cargo arriving from Vasquez was agricultural, but some of the specialty foods were easy to bruise. He couldn't imagine that the cargo pods would be manhandled like that. Another jolt almost sent him to the floor, and from behind him, Colby heard a sound no one in space ever wants to hear: a hissing.

All of the vines connected to the bulkheads lifted up in unison.

Colby spun around, trying to pinpoint the hissing, but it wasn't in the bridge.

"Stay here, girl!" he shouted, bolting for the passage leading to the ship's rear. The hissing grew louder, and he could feel the movement of air. And then he saw it. The tip of a ceralloy blade had cut into the ship. Air whistled around it.

Tiny, overlapping, green scales flowed along the ship's walls trying to seal around the puncture, some kind of automated algae that struggled to coat the cargo drone's arms and immobilize them. They failed when, as if shifting its grip, the prong moved, making the hole a little larger. What had been a soft hissing became a roar, pulling at Colby. If the drone's grasping arm moved again, there would be an explosive decompression.

"Duke!"

Colby turned and ran back, fighting the rush of air. Duke was whining, her voice sounding tinny as the air became thinner. She ran up to him, trying to jump into his arms.

Even without a catastrophic evacuation, he knew his time was limited. He had a minute, maybe a little more, to figure their way out of this mess. The ship jolted again, almost knocking him down.

The locker!

Colby grabbed the struggling Duke, then dragged her to the locker. If he could get inside and close it, then he'd at least have that much O2 to breathe, which was a heck of a lot better than trying to breathe vacuum.

He hit the door release three, four times, as dark spots danced across his vision. Finally, the door opened. There wasn't enough room for him and Duke with the alien's body there. He put Duke down, then yanked the body with all his might, pulling it out, tearing it free of the vines that had held it and flailed to continue in that purpose. Gasping, he fell on his ass in the process, the plant carcass sprawled on top of him. He lay there a moment dazed.

Get with it, Edson!

He pushed the body off him, then grabbed Duke by the scruff her neck and threw her into the locker. He pulled the boss plant's severed head out and tossed it to the deck, then jumped in, pushing Duke to the back.

"Close, damn you!" he gasped, punching every square centimeter near the opening.

He was entering hypoxia. He recognized the signs: confusion, sweating, wheezing. If there'd been a reflective surface anywhere on this damn ship he didn't doubt that it would show his skin color somewhere between blue and cherry red. Like all Marines, he'd undergone vacuum training, and as part of that, he'd been sent into never-never-land in a training chamber. He'd hoped he'd never feel that again.

The ship lurched, more powerfully then before, and Colby was thrown and pinned against the back of the locker, face first in a mass of leafy vegetation. His body ached in a familiar way as gee forces reminded him of the difference between weight and mass. The ship was accelerating. His dog whimpered, though whether from her own hypoxia or the extra gees he couldn't tell.

"Sorry Duke," he coughed, feeling her warm body at his feet. "The drone must be dragging us downward, for all the good it'll do us."

She stopped whining and hugged him back, which made him feel good. They were going to go out together.

She hugged me?

He managed to turn despite the forces holding him to the wall. It wasn't Duke. The same vines that had wrapped around the alien's corpse had now latched onto to him and were holding him fast. He knew he should fight them, but he couldn't. His mouth opened as he gasped for air, but there just wasn't any. He straightened back up and feebly pushed at the opening, trying once more to close the door.

And then he was out of energy. This was the end, he knew.

Surprisingly, he wasn't angry, he wasn't panicking. He felt a wave of lassitude sweep over him as he gave up.

In his last moments, he started hallucinating. Sergeant Warshowki, his first DI, appeared, yelling at him to get up. Colby just giggled. The head of the alien scurried across the floor towards the control panels, dozens of tiny plant fingers having emerged from its neck to carry it along. He giggled again and his world went dark.

Interlude I: Per Capita Perspective

A frigid torpor gripped the Gardener, a lethargy it only understood as it broke through the edge of it like a questing root easing through clay soil. Bits of memory—glimpses somewhere between acquisition and true consolidation—taunted its awareness. Meat had entered its vessel. Meat with tools and weapons. They had attacked. Its attempt to neutralize the pair of primitives had failed and. . . one of them. . . severed its cranium from the ambulatory caudex it had fashioned rotations earlier. That accounted for both the disjuncture of memory and the torpor. The brutality of their incursion had shocked the Gardener into quiescence. Before it could recover, whether by design or random chance or simple Meat destiny, they had returned the pieces to the cold storage of the craft's navigation locker where the waiting vines exuded much-needed and healing oxygen even as the lower temperatures slowed its restoration and pushed its awareness into oblivion.

Until it hadn't. Circumstances had altered, and quickly. Its recovering sensorium as yet possessed only limited visual processing, like seeing through a thick layer of unremitting cellulose, which coupled with the steady warming of its core was enough to recognize that it no longer lay within the alcove. A silhouette, possibly that of one of the Meat creatures, wrestled a smaller, quadruped form into the space, batting at the indiscriminate vines that sought to embrace them both.

Audition returned and brought the whistle of escaping air. Escaping to where? Its elegant vessel rested comfortably in a forest clearing. And yet. . . as more and more of its cognitive processing came back to it, the Gardener understood. The vessel was not at rest, not on the planet at all, was in fact in space and damaged, possibly hulled.

It strained and pushed at the ganglia bundle that had once connected it with a functional trunk and limbs. They descended from the slit just above the point of its neck wound, trembling as they adapted to serve as ambulatory roots. By whatever fluke, the Meat had managed to launch its ship into space. Necessity demanded it interface with controls, initiate repairs, and expunge the pests.

The vessel jerked, rolling on an axis that should never have known rotation, and accelerated along a vector that was impossible for it. The Gardener skittered across the floor, re-evaluating priorities and aiming itself toward one of the ship's backup seed supply compartments along the edge of the far wall. The compartment served double duty as an emergency pod, existing to launch an assortment of supplies in the event of absolute catastrophe. Under such contingencies the Gardener's own navigation pod could also launch as a life pod. As the rising cry of dwindling air demonstrated, the situation had reached that extreme, but there was insufficient time to eject the Meat from its escape route. Nor did it require such action. In its current form, the supply pod would serve.

Pressing a root ganglion into the wall, it accessed the vessel's systems to open a slit into its intended destination.

The access was granted, but even as the Gardener slipped within an alien clamor reverberated through it. An outside force had accessed the vessel's systems!

Impossible!

The system had been tainted, and yet the telltales of a Mechanical infestation were not present—which explained why the defenses it had crafted against such an attack had not activated. No, it was unthinkable. There was only Meat on the vessel. Meat did not possess the sophistication or technical savvy to communicate with spacecraft. And yet. . . as the Gardener communed with the vessel it had nurtured from a seed, it read the evidence that they had lifted from the planet's surface, exited its gravity well, and passed through some spacial anomaly that had left it in an uncharted location before it had been attacked by a robotic tool of limited intellectual capacity.

Meat. Meat capable of space travel, capable of movement between stellar bodies. Impossible!

And yet. . . clearly possible. The Gardener compiled the horrifying ramifications, bracing itself against the cushioned sleeves of supplies making up the pod's emergency seedbank. It abandoned any possibility of saving its vessel even as it abandoned the vessel itself. The greater need was to get away, determine its location, and get word back to its people. Meat was loose in the galaxy, with the full range and promise of ruination that Meat delivered on any world where it evolved.

Indifferent to increased acceleration, it launched the newly purposed life pod, bringing its rudimentary navigation systems to life, relieved to find no taint of Meat present. Crude visual sensors showed the shattered shape of its once beautiful vessel gripped and pinched by a robotic tool that dragged it toward a distant mud-red sphere at speed.

The Gardener consulted a manifest of its supplies and allowed itself a moment of relief. Assuming the planet wasn't too distant, assuming it held even a modicum of friendly soil, it could grow the tools it would need, fashion a body appropriate to its demands, and do what had to be done.

The desire to tend its own garden could wait. Meat, thinking Meat, threatened everything that set down roots or yearned for simple sunshine. That threat would be eliminated first and foremost.

□

Part II: Home is Where They Have to Take You In

A fractal of frames slowly formed in Colby's mind. Each tiny image revealed a progression towards an immense facility of some sort, but from a slightly different perspective. Each frame moved independently from all of the others, in different vectors, spins, and rotations that weren't limited to three dimensions. Colby knew it was a dream, but it still made him nauseous, and he thought he was going to lose the emergency rations he'd eaten with Topeka before leaving Vasquez.

Two sounds started to register as well: a low moaning and a higher pitched whining. With his growing discomfort, it took a moment to realize that the moaning was coming from him. And that meant the whining was. . .

Duke?

He tried to reach out to her, but couldn't move. A million hands conspired to restrain him. They held him back, keeping him from her for no purpose he could fathom. As a young lieutenant, he'd often had nightmares of being in an assault on an enemy position, with his Marines leading the way, only to feel as if he was trying to run through quicksand. He feared not being able to make it to the assault and being branded a coward, but no matter how hard he tried, he could not break free from the quicksand's grip.

Now, the same feeling of frustration and fear swept over him. Duke needed him, and he wasn't able to get to her. The thousands of images, most of the fuzzily out-of-focus building, relentlessly pounded into his brain, too much for him to take. The dream demons were not going to let him comfort his dog.

Even in his sleep, his body revolted. His stomach heaved, the acidic bile burning his throat. He wasn't sure if he dream-vomited, or if it had been real. He struggled to turn his head, afraid of suffocating in his sleep, but his brain simply shut down, and he sunk back into the welcome embrace of oblivion.

****

Oblivion ended. Time resumed with little indication of how long it had been held in abeyance. As Colby started to resurface from the depths of darkness, the myriad of images appeared again. As before, most of them centered on a large structure, as if each was a feed created by a tiny camera on an independently operated bot of some sort. Like he was a security guard monitoring a building at night, but instead of 20 wall-mounted spy-eyes showing different areas in a building, he had thousands of aerial feeds, all showing the same thing, each from a slightly different angle or distance.

The images themselves were odd, with deeper, more vivid colors in the blues and purples, with a lack of reds and yellows. Colby was familiar with the full range of military scanners, and the images reminded him of what ultra-violet surveillance gear produced.

Nausea threatened him again, but he fought that back down. His mouth and throat still burned from before.

Wait a minute. Did I really puke? Or am I back in the same dream?

Colby had been subject to recurring dreams since his forced resignation from the Corps, but not like this. It was as if whatever he was dreaming before had just picked up where he'd left it. He didn't understand what was going on, and it was hard to concentrate while being bombarded with sensory overload.

Control yourself, Edson.

The sheer number of inputs was overwhelming, but the overall concept of controlling different inputs was not anything new. As a leader of Marines, he'd had to manage individual inputs from his Marines as well as scanners and comms with higher headquarters. It had been difficult at first, even with only the thirty-nine Marines and corpsmen in his platoon. But with the help of his command implant and hours of practice, his mind learned how to make sense of everything. As he became more senior and had more Marines in his command, he'd increased his capacity for comprehension. But the thousands of inputs coming at him now was an order of magnitude more than he'd ever had to monitor before. And yet. . . once he'd awakened enough to understand what was happening—if not actually what he was receiving—it was clear that his unconscious mind had clued in sooner. Based on his familiarity with the general concept, it had begun rewiring the patterns of his synapses, rerouting the organization of the feeds so that, with the help of his implant, he started to have a sense of the overall picture.

He was treating this as reality, not a dream, and that insight provided the final push, letting him focus on only a few inputs chosen at random, flicking from one subset to another and another. The building in the images had the Spartan look of a commercial processing center, like the—

Hell, I'm on New Mars.

It came rushing back to him. He'd taken the alien ship through the wormhole. The cargo drone had damaged the ship, and it had bled air. His last-ditch effort to save Duke and himself had worked, somehow, but while he was out cold, the drone had taken the ship to one of the planet's processing centers, along with what were probably hundreds, if not thousands, of other cargo containers.

Colby opened his eyes—to nothingness. He felt a moment of panic, but ironically, it was the onslaught of other images that kept him grounded. With a mental flipping of the switch, a trick he'd mastered over the years of battlesuit telemetry, he compartmentalized the inputs, shoving them to the side to focus on his own senses. He still couldn't see anything, but it was now simply darkness, not a loss of vision. Which in turn allowed him to register his other senses again.

Nearby, Duke softly whined, and she struggled, pressing herself against his side.

"Easy, girl. I'm here with you. It's going to be OK."

She seemed to quiet down, but that could have been his imagination. What wasn't his imagination was the itch that started to take over his senses, threatening to shut them down much as the visual inputs had before.

Or maybe it was—he didn't know. It didn't matter if it was real or his imagination, it was driving him batty. It was as if a horde of cockroaches were crawling over him. He tried to lift his arm to scratch, which in turn reminded him that he was still being held fast.

He heaved, struggling with all his strength, but while there was some give, he couldn't manage any real movement. After two solid minutes of effort, he gave up. His body was still trying to make sense of everything, and he didn't want to waste energy on a futile attempt to break free.

"I've been immobilized and I've got who knows what being shot into my mind," he said aloud, a technique he'd picked up when first learning to use his implant and feeds as a lieutenant.

When faced with too much input, it helped to verbalize his thoughts. His voice was working fine, and as it had so many years ago, speaking allowed him to hone in on the specifics that defined a situation.

"I'm on the ship, probably on New Mars. I'm getting feeds from somewhere, too many of them to handle."

The feeds started encroaching again, and he hurriedly continued, "Most of all, I'm still alive, so I can affect what is going on. First thing first is to figure out why I'm getting the feeds."

He tried to focus on a single input, but then the bulk of them started pressing down on his soul.

"One at a time, Edson, one at a time. That one, right there. I'm only looking at you, so reveal your secrets. I'm ignoring the rest for now, so only you."

His implant was second nature to him after so many years, and even if it had been a long time since he'd pushed its capabilities to full operation mode, his mind slipped into it like a pair of well-worn shoes. The rest of the feeds remained, as did the sounds of Duke's and his breathing, the itch on his skin, even the sound of his voice, but his chosen feed seemed to expand and come into focus.

"Shit, it's more of the plants!" he said, as everything whirled back into the jumble of impressions.

"Bring it back, Edson." He forced everything into place and brought his chosen feed back to the fore.

When first confronted with the thousands of images, the large building had been all he'd noticed. But now, with his attention on just one feed, while the structure still occupied the foreground of the image he could make out details in the background, a background that resolved into a sea of plant soldiers. The colors were off from what he'd seen on Vasquez, but there was no mistaking the shape and movement. With a mental command, he released the feed, and it retreated to join the rest of the confusing mass.

"I did this," he said. "I brought them back through the wormhole with me. Somehow, they were in the ship, and now they're loose."

An image? Memory? of the boss plant's head scuttling across the deck on tiny legs came to his mind. He thought it had been a hallucination brought on by hypoxia, like Sergeant Warshowki yelling at him, but what if it had been real? Was the thing somehow alive and now waging war on New Mars?

If so, that made Colby a traitor to humankind. Sure, he'd been railroaded into resigning his commission, but if he'd just abetted an alien invasion, he deserved whatever punishment would be meted out.

"I've got to fix this."

His own fate was the hangman's noose, but that was irrelevant in the big picture. He was still a Marine, a loyal servant of mankind, and he was going to do anything he could to avert this catastrophe.

He pulled another of the feeds to the fore, this time not having to speak. A mental shrug was his only acknowledgment that this was getting easier. His implant excelled at adapting, filling in gaps to make the system work.

His new point of view was at the wall of the building itself. Leafy green tendrils reached up, attached themselves with a wet click to the walls, and started to pull.

"Click?" he said. "Did I feel that or hear that?"

A crack opened up in the wall, grabbing his attention. Within moments, the crack was a gap, and his host? slipped in. With a start he realized what he should have known all along: the feeds were coming from the plants. He was seeing the world through the horde of plant soldiers. Colby understood what he was experiencing, although he'd only known it on a much smaller scale. When he hitched a ride with a Marine in a battlesuit, it was through the Marine's sensors and cam feeds. This wasn't so different. If he concentrated, he could sense everything around the plant soldier, a full three-sixty. No, more than a three-sixty, a complete sphere around it.

He started to get nauseous again and had to pull back. It had been bad enough when faced with a bee eye's kaleidoscope of thousands of views, but now, he had full environmental awareness from a multitude of sources, and worse still, they all that overlapped one another.

He threw up again, a poor effort that was mostly stomach acid. He spit several times, clearing his mouth. A moment later, he could feel the spit drop back down on his neck from where it had fallen from the locker's ceiling.

If he was going to do anything, he had to find a way to block some of the sensory input. Even with his implant integrating better, there was just too much for him to process. He just didn't know how to do that.

"Maybe the security shields?" he asked, his burning throat turning his words into a rasp.

His implant was the pinnacle of current technology, an amazing piece of gear, powered by a tiny long-life battery implanted in his sinuses. As tiny as the current draw was, however, it was possible for a sophisticated enemy to hack his implant, which could obviously have terrible consequences in a battle. That was why implants like his were not only heavily shielded, but he could erect firewalls at will.

He pulled up his collection of firewalls and selected FC-90, which had an hourglass neck that allowed the passage of a limited amount of data. He slapped the firewall over the feeds, then hesitantly opened the flow. It wasn't perfect, but it helped. The onslaught dropped from overwhelming to barely manageable.

Feeling a little more confident, he found another plant soldier already inside the building and zeroed in on it. Within a split second, he was the soldier. It was his arms that were tearing apart a piece of machinery, ripping pressure rollers right off of their cradle. Another plant pulled one of the heavy cerasteel pieces out of its grasp and started to bend it in two.

His plant reached for a control, and a spark jumped across, zapping it.

"Yow!" Colby yelled. "Wait, how the hell did that happen?"

Colby was not feeling everything the plant touched, but he experienced that shock. At least, he thought he did. His fingers were still tingling, and it sure felt real.

His implant had high-level haptic controls imbedded into it. With enough practice—and Colby had had more than enough over the course of his career—he could control machines with what was essentially a mental touch. It was as if his fingers were on physical controls. He could virtually feel pressure, vibration, temperature, and other sensations without ever actually touching the object.

"Wait a minute. If there is a haptic connection here, then can I control it the same way I can control a drone?"

He jumped back into the feeds and his previous host. It was attacking the base of the control panel. Colby reached out to it, taking his virtual hand and grabbing the thing's real hand. Nothing happened. The green plant arm passed through his virtual hand as if it was, well, virtual.

"Shit, Edson, concentrate!"

He tried again, this time building up the hand, adding bones, tendons, and ligaments. The plant soldier's arm might have hesitated a moment, but it wasn't stopped, and it tore another piece of the machinery apart.

"What am I doing wrong?" he asked.

He tried several more tacks, even running through his Troubleshooting checklist, but nothing was working. The machine, whatever it was, was soon turned into scrap, and the plant soldier moved to the next one.

Colby switched to another plant soldier but didn't have any more success. He knew he was making tiny adjustments in their actions, but not enough to stop any of them from destroying the factory.

Where're the facility's security forces? Are they going to just ignore this?

The factories were the lifeblood of New Mars, and to much of the Republic. Most were automated, but still, there were Marines and local security forces on the planet for a reason. They should be reacting to the assault.

Colby paused from his efforts and widened the awareness of his host so he could simply take in the scene, hoping to see signs of the cavalry riding in to save the day. All he saw was destruction. The entire wall of the factory was gone, and a good half of the machinery destroyed. All of the plants were working with a single purpose.

Well, all except one. A single solder was whirling around aimlessly, knocking into the others. It stopped and stood still for a moment, then lashed out erratically with a ropy arm. . . at the same time that Duke jerked at his side.

What?

His fingers were not restrained, and he could feel Duke's warm body. He pushed out into her, and she jerked within her restraints. At the same time, the crazy plant soldier jerked.

"Duke, Duke, who's a good girl?"

The plant soldier stopped, then wiggled.

"Duke, are you controlling that plant? Are you?"

He pushed harder into her with his fingers, producing a yelp. Immediately, the plant solder stopped wiggling and marched to join the rest at the nearest machine.

He couldn't believe what he'd seen. His eyes told him that the soldier and Duke had somehow been attached, but his mind screamed that was ridiculous. And it was ridiculous. A dog couldn't control an enemy soldier, could she?

Unless this really was a dream brought about in his last seconds of life in a hypoxia-induced death, it sure looked like the two had been connected. It made a perverse degree of sense. Somehow, he was connected to the plant soldiers as they rampaged. Why not Duke? They were both inside a womb of sorts in the locker. Colby had the sneaking suspicion that the ship's tendrils had not only kept them alive, but somehow plugged them to the plant ecosystem. They'd been connected to the command and control.

And it hit him. Duke had stopped the plant soldier in its tracks. Colby had been trying to stop an arm by simply holding it back. He should have been doing as Duke did and become the host, for lack of a better term.

He turned back inwards to his host. Instead of trying to control its movements, he pictured himself sinking into it, being subsumed by it. Nothing happened, but he wasn't going to give up. If a dog could do it, so could a human. He closed off every possible input he could, seeing himself sink into the quicksand of the soldier. This was too reminiscent of his nightmares, so he changed that to sinking into a warm bath. He could feel the plant's very being, but he could not find a way in. He adjusted, shifted, changed the force of his projections, and suddenly, something opened up, and he started to fall in. . . and immediately clawed for freedom.

He'd felt himself being controlled, instead of him doing the controlling. The plant mind was not like anything he'd experienced nor imagined. It was so. . . alien. It wasn't what he'd imagined a science fiction hive mind to be, but it sure wasn't human, and that scared him to the quick. He'd almost been taken over by it.

Marines don't quit, however, and Colby knew he had to do something. But what? He'd pictured himself sinking into the plant. What if he reversed that image? What if the plant sunk into him? Or if he surrounded it?

He formed a new image, one of his body flowing around the plant, taking it in like an amoeba eating a bacterium. He'd already formed a type of resonance with this plant soldier, and far quicker than he'd expected, he'd drawn the plant in. Colby was still Colby, and he thought he was in control of the plant. The soldier was attacking another machine, and Colby reached out with his mind with a command to stop. The soldier hesitated, but after a moment commenced again.

Frustrated, Colby sent out a powerful order, a mental scream. The soldier stopped dead, ropy limbs still grasping the machine. Another plant pulled the machine parts from his soldier, and still, it remained motionless.

Carefully, Colby withdrew, waiting for the plant to start in on the attack again. It remained motionless. If he could, he'd have raised a fist into the air in triumph.

There had to be more than a thousand of the plant soldiers inside the ruins of the factory, and Colby sensed that there were far more destroying other factories. It was too much for him to grasp the magnitude of what he was trying to do, so he refused to think about it. Every journey began with a single step.

He shifted to another host to begin the process again.

****

"Stop that plant," Colby sent, then waited to see what would happen.

After an hour, he'd only stopped thirty plants from their rampage of destruction. It became clear that he was fighting a losing battle, and his finger in the dyke wasn't going to hold back the ocean. He had to change tactics, and this was his attempt to do more.

His implant was continually improving the interface with each interaction, and with a specific command, he was hoping he could get soldier to fight soldier. If he was successful, that would make his impact that much greater. Instead of a single plant standing still, he would take out two: one being held, and the other doing the holding.

In the back of his mind, he kept wondering about the boss plant. Topeka had taken off the thing's head, but he now believed what he'd seen with the head scuttling across the ship's bridge. Something had started the plant army on their rampage here on New Mars. Was its objective the same as back on Vasquez? Was it orchestrating this attack? And if it was out there controlling the assault, why hadn't it ordered any of the stopped soldiers back into battle? All good questions, but Colby lacked sufficient intel for more than guesswork, besides which his immediate focus was consumed by taking over the plant soldiers.

Ordering one soldier to attack another was different that simply stopping it. His target plant reached over and wrapped up the soldier next to it. That one kept reaching for the last pieces of the machine it had been dismantling, but Colby's plant was like an octopus. They both teetered for a moment before falling over. They lay intertwined on the grounds, ropy plant arms twisted in each other's grip.

"Two for one," Colby said.

Duke answered with a piteous yelp. He knew she had to be confused and scared, but there wasn't much he could do about it.

Unless I can get one of the soldiers to come back and open the locker and free us?

He'd tried several times to free a foot and start hunting for the hatch release, but he hadn't come close. He knew he was in the locker for the long haul unless he could figure out a way to be rescued.

But if I get out of here, can I still control them?

Whatever was holding them was probably what allowed him and Duke to interface with the plant soldiers. It boggled the mind that two different forms of life could connect like that, but the universe was filled with amazing things, and the proof was right there in front of him.

For the moment, he and Duke were safe, and he could control the plant soldiers, so it was probably better to stand pat and create more havoc. He checked on his quisling, which had managed to tear off one of its opponent's arms, but was now in danger of losing one of its own. He was hoping it could make short shrift of the other, but as the two combatants slowly maneuvered for the upper hand, he realized that wasn't going to happen anytime soon, if at all. He gave it another command to attack, figuring it wouldn't hurt to reinforce his last command, then withdrew, looking for his next target.

He was able to take over this one in less than a minute, and it unhesitantly turned from a half-destroyed fabricator of some sort to fall upon the soldier next to it. It took another minute for the victim to seem to realize what was happening and turn to face its ally-turned-enemy. None of the other soldiers seemed to notice the pair and they wrapped each other up in mortal combat.

As his implant fine-tuned the process, the time to take over a soldier became less and less. By his tenth "grab," as he began to think of it, the process took about thirty seconds. The fabricator that had been this group of soldiers' target was out-of-action, but no more damage was being done.

Colby felt a thrill of victory before he widened his perceptions. This factory had to still have a couple of hundred as of yet undamaged machines, and there were hundreds of plant soldiers still bent on destroying every last one of them.

"No time to admire your handiwork, Edson. Get your ass back to work."

****

Just over thirty minutes later, Colby had set another fifty-six soldiers against their brethren, so 111 were out of the demolition sweepstakes. It was only 111 because one of the ones Colby'd attacked had managed to tear off all the arms of the one he had taken over. It limped back to join the others while its attacker tried to inchworm-hump after it. Colby paused to watch the victor for a moment, he needed the break. His head ached with the onset of a killer migraine, just like the ones he sometimes had when first learning to use his implant.

The tips of his fingers rested on what was probably Duke's haunch, and the contact was an anchor. He was sure she appreciated his touch as well. He wasn't connecting with her like he was with the plant soldiers he'd commandeered. But there was some sort of connection going on, just the tiniest bit of backsurge in the tendrils that held them both fast.

He breathed deep, and took control of the limping soldier, ready to send it to attack one of the others, but with only half of a single arm left, he realized that the thing couldn't do much damage. He was about to shift to another soldier when a blinding light filled his head, a flash of intense pain flooding him for an instant before it was gone.

What the . . .

The jolt had been a flash, almost too short to feel, but his nerves trembled as if remembering pain. His headache intensified, and he struggled trying to bring his hands up to his temples.

He forced himself to concentrate, trying to select another frame to figure out what had happened. It was easier to slip into his previous captive, and from it, he could see the limping soldier, or rather, what was left of it. Bits and pieces were strewn haphazardly around the floor and walls, a green mist hovering in the still air where his host had stood.

A streak of red light flashed past his/the plant soldier's field of view, and one of the soldiers tearing into another piece of machinery exploded into a thousand bits of plant. More green mist bloomed over the spot.

Colby knew that flash for laser light. Specifically, the laser from a M88 rifle, and that could mean only one thing—the Marines had finally arrived!

Several more lasers reached out, exploding the soldiers. The lasers weren't doing the damage—they were merely the spotting tool, like an old-fashioned tracer round. The M88 was a microwave rifle, sending out two megajoules joules at 20 GHz in .25-second pulses.

It was a perfect weapon for rapidly heating water—and objects which contained water tended to come apart with extreme prejudice. Plant soldiers evidently contained a lot of water.

An M88 could fire five hundred times on a single charge, taking only five seconds to recharge the capacitor between shots. As he expected, five seconds after the initial volley, another one reached out, exploding six more plants into mist.

"Get some!" he shouted, his voice muffled by the vines holding him.

The soldiers might have been single-minded in tearing the factory apart, but they were still soldiers, plant-things or not. Almost as one, they turned to face the threat and surged forward.

Colby shifted his perspective, and a platoon of Marines was entering the building in perfect assault formation through the destroyed back walls. His heart raced with excitement, and he longed to be out there, a lieutenant again, leading the assault. In their mech battlesuits, Marines were a menacing sight to most bad guys, but to him, they were comfort, pride, and. . . yes, love, all rolled into one.

He needed to let the Marines know what they were facing. He tried to pull them up through his implant, but it was like barreling down a highway only to hit a stone wall. Nothing went through, and he wasn't sure why. He started a troubleshooting worm to work on it, then turned his attention back to the fight.

Another volley of lasers cut down the soldiers in the front of the rush towards the Marines. The soldier next to Colby's exploded, the force knocking his viewpoint plant to its knees? Lower extremity? A wave of panic roared through him. He'd just had one host under his control killed, and it was not something he wanted to go through again. He shifted his focus away from the action, jumping to one of the soldiers outside the building.

"Damn!" was all he could say.

He'd been focusing on the factory, knowing there was much more going on, but not to what extent. Every factory or warehouse in sight was flattened or close to it. Thousands. . . tens of thousands of plant soldiers were pouring out of the wreckage, converging on what looked to be two rifle companies, about two hundred Marines. Three crew-served M280 particle-beam cannons were spewing nano-pulse beams of death, mowing down the plant soldiers like so much genwheat in the path of an unrelenting harvester.

The toll on the soldiers was frightening. A thousand had already died, the particulate flurry of their remains giving rise to that green mist. More frightening, however, was that the wave of vegetable bodies inched closer and closer to the Marines.

"You are too dispersed!" Colby yelled out to the commander, even knowing no one could hear him.

Almost immediately, the platoon that had been entering the building started to pull back, and for a moment, Colby watched in shock.

Can I control the Marines, too? No, that's impossible. The commander was taught the same as I was and is seeing the same thing.

Marines are taught to take the fight to the enemy, to seek them out and destroy them. But with thousands of plant soldiers eagerly advancing on the Marines, sometimes the best offense was a good defense. By creating a strong defensive perimeter, the Marines could employ interlocking and mutually supporting fields of fire, creating an impenetrable wall of energy.

In theory.

The M280s were devastating weapons, but they were big, bulky, and not very maneuverable—not so much due to the cannon itself, but from the powerpack. Particle beam weapons were energy hogs, better suited for tank bodies or Navy ships. The cooling coils alone were larger than the projector tubes. For a crew-served weapon, the Achilles heel was changing out the power cell. In normal operations, a three-cannon section would rotate the power cell switch-out so at least two cannons were up at all times. This time, the numbers of plant soldiers closing in were so huge, the firing was so intense, that the choreography was interrupted, and two of the weapons had gone offline at the same time.

With a huge gap, the Marine riflemen couldn't keep up with the mass of the charging plant soldiers, and they reached their Little Big Top, breaking into the line of Marines. Monomolecular blades took over from rifles as the fight devolved into hand-to-branch combat, but while the M88 exploded the plant soldiers, cutting them was far less effective. Even missing arms or with huge chunks taken out of the bodies, the plant soldiers kept up the attack like zombies seeking brains.

Hell, do something, Edson!

He'd been so caught up in the fight, switching from one host to the other, that he'd forgotten that he could still affect the battle. At least fifty of the plant soldiers were amongst the Marines, and several Marines were down. One lay still on the ground, left arm gone while three plant soldiers were tearing the cerroalloy ISP armor apart. The same armor that could withstand a 105mm artillery round was like papier-mâché to the plants' relentless strength.

A Marine stepped up, and with a tremendous blow from the monomolecular blade extending from the battlesuit's arm, sliced one of the soldiers attacking the downed Marine in half, separating the lower ambulatory "legs" from the rest. Even so, it still kept prying apart bits of battlesuit.

Colby swooped in, a hawk on a rabbit, flooding one of the three soldiers, and took control. His host released its hold on the broken edge of the battlesuit's chest carapace, and at Colby's direction, shifted to the other fully functional soldier, intertwining its arms in the other's, immobilizing it.

Marines closed in, firing kinetic handguns, which didn't bother Colby much, but also swinging bladed arms, which hurt like hell. What had been simply vague impressions of pain were now much more pronounced. As his implant's control of the interface had improved, the tactile transfer had grown stronger as well.

Colby stayed in place, however, absorbing the pain until he felt the soldier's remaining arms starting to lose their grip before withdrawing. He didn't want to risk being connected when the thing died.

His skin still tingled, as if he'd been cut himself. He took a couple of deep breaths, then dove back into the fray. He pulled two more soldiers off Marines before the soldiers inside the lines started exploding again.

About freaking time!

A Marine battlesuit could take a fairly good pounding from a microwave weapon, and getting "hosed down" was an accepted course of action when the enemy was intermixed with Marines. The cannons must be back online, so the Marines who'd been concentrating on keeping more plant soldiers from reaching them could focus on their buddies and clear the lines.

Colby shifted outside the Marine lines to one of the soldiers in the back of the mob. What had been thousands was far, far fewer as more and more were cut down. That green mist was now a thick green fog, which was not good for the Marines. Particle beams were amazing weapons, but they lost power through electrostatic bloom, and that effect was heightened with particulates in the air. The cannon beams cut the air with a shimmering glow, but that glowing meant energy was being diverted.

Some of the plants around him didn't have the same fervor, if he was reading plant body language correctly. A couple hundred broke off from the rear of the pack, including his host. For a moment, he thought they were quitting the field of battle, but no, there was a purpose to the movement. They had not lost their fervor--this group was maneuvering to flank the Marines. If the body of plant soldiers were being controlled by the boss plant, then the boss must have realized it was wasting bodies, and was changing tactics.

These were not mindless automatons—well, perhaps the soldiers themselves were, but not the force guiding them. That made them much more dangerous.

Colby jumped to one of the lead soldiers and commanded it to divert, hoping the others would follow. They didn't. They bypassed his captured host and kept marching. He was about to order his host to tackle one of the others, but it wouldn't do much good. The fight was well out of his hands.

Instead, he turned his host around and sent it to the back of the main body where it would hopefully become a Marine target. He pulled out of it, then tried to digest what the remaining thousands of frames showed him. If he could see a pattern in what the plants were doing, then get that to the commander, then he'd be contributing . . .

Beside him, Duke yelped piteously and struggled for a moment, before settling into a whine.

"Calm down, girl. I'm here," he said, stroking her side with the tips of his fingers, a tiny motion, but one that seemed to help her.

He wondered what had set her off before it hit him. He'd felt what it was like to be in a host when it was killed. He'd wager Duke had been out there, inside one of the soldiers when the Marines had destroyed it. For a moment, his anger rose against the Marines, the bastards, the—

What the hell, Edson? What are you thinking?

He'd never, ever, thought bad about the Marines, not even when he was being cashiered out of the service. He'd hated a few other Marines during his career, and he hated Vice-Minister Greenstein with a passion, but that wasn't the Corps. He loved the Corps, and he felt an overwhelming sense of guilt over what he'd just felt.

How could that have happened?

Something taking over a large proportion of the frames caught his attention, diverting him from his guilt. It was the Marines, launching into their attack.

"Oo-rah!" he shouted, wondering if that was still from his heart.

The Marines poured in tight company wedges designed to pierce the remaining plants with maximum firepower to the front and flanks. One company headed to cut off the plants that were trying to envelope them. Colby should have known that the commander would have been aware of the situation and had recognized the same thing he had.

"Just let him fight. You're not in command," he muttered.

With the cannons remaining back to deliver supporting fire, the Marines tore through the diminished numbers, blasting plant soldiers into bits and pieces. The green fog of death intensified and more soldiers were vaporized, but as the Marines closed in, their weapons kept spitting out death. The two companies were machines, killing machines. The plants didn't have a chance.

More and more of his frames winked out, and he began to lose his situational awareness of what was happening. There were too many gaps, but that was a good thing. It meant the Marines were winning. Within an hour, he was down to seven frames, seven left from the thousands or tens of thousands—he'd never been able to determine just how many there'd been. From what he could tell, these were from seven immobile soldiers, probably wounded too much to continue to fight.

One was at what looked to be the old defensive position. Colby took a chance and slipped around it, taking it captive. He tried to get it to move, but while he could sense it trying to respond, nothing happened. It lacked arms it could move, or legs stalks to escape. It couldn't even wriggle its body. From the larger pieces of green chunks around it, Colby thought it had to be one of those that had reached the Marine lines only to be chopped down by the blades.

At least its senses worked. Colby slipped back out, but gave its frame his primary attention. A few Marines were within its sensory range, beyond which was the thick green fog of dead plant bits. A breeze picked up, slowly blowing the fog away and revealing the Marines, like monsters emerging from the schlockiest holovid, as they returned. The sight was impressive, and Colby hoped the surveillance drones that had to be flying overhead were recording this. Images like these convinced young men and women to enlist.

But something was wrong. Some of the Marines were limping, their battlesuits giving uncharacteristic lurches. Marine battlesuits tended to either work or not. They could be blasted to smithereens by heavy kinetics, they could be fried by energy weapons that overcame their shielding, but they didn't tend to get merely damaged. Once the armor or shielding failed, it was usually a catastrophic kill.

As he watched the Marines form up, more and more were in obvious distress. Colby was baffled. He switched among his remaining seven feeds, but the one from the defensive position provided the best view, and that revealed nothing. More and more of the Marines lurched about, and several platoons moved into defensive positions, weapons outboard.

One Marine stopped dead in midstride, then another. Others froze as well. Within minutes a good third of the Marines had become unmoving statues. A battlesuit was effective because it both protected a Marine from fire while allowing the Marine to close with and destroy the enemy. Without maneuverability, it was just a pillbox waiting for the enemy to outmaneuver it. Colby wasn't surprised when first one, then in a rush, Marines were molting, getting out of their suits. Wary Marines, now armed with the smaller man-packed weapons, took positions by their dead battlesuits, facing outboard, and probably wondering just what the hell had happened. Colby wondered that as well.

The two companies of Marines had won a decisive battle, overcoming a veritable horde of enemy plant soldiers with what might have been a single friendly casualty. Now, after the battle, the Marines had somehow been stripped of their biggest advantage.

The Marines had won the battle, but from what Colby could see, it was a Pyrrhic victory.

☐

Interlude II: A New World, A New Infestation

The Gardener's supply-pod-turned-escape-vessel skimmed across the atmosphere of the mud-red planet, venting velocity and attempting to limit temperature extremes as it descended. The limited sensory details it could access revealed a barren world, one that would take thousands of revolutions of effort and planning to transform into a garden. Robotic vessels appeared to come and go from a single point, a slight deviation from the mud, presumably the destination for the unthinkable, space-faring Meat. As terrifying as that prospect was, it was also the only place to have the living resources needed to restore itself, or to grow the tools needed to protect itself from the Meat.

It adjusted its course and fell from the sky. There was no way to know what technological capabilities this new Meat had mastered, and the Gardener's best course was to act like an insignificant bit of space debris, some remnant that was left from a larger chunk that had all but burned up in reentry. Moments before striking down, its sensors discerned the shapes of artificial structures much like the invading Meat had built within its garden world, but also thousands of vast containers, each easily as large as its former vessel. Several of the containers were open and its sensors detected organic material, much of it similar to the material contaminating the garden it had recently purged.

It could work with that.

At the last instant, the Gardener manipulated mathematical constructs, twisting gravity and velocity. Its pod still crashed, but did not crater the ground or destroy its cargo. Moreover, it had positioned itself near one of the containers. It reviewed its stock, reviewed the plans it had made, and released a plume of tiny seeds high into the air. A portion would enter the container, take root within the material it found there. In less than a rotation of this muddy world this new seeding would yield the Gardener's first wave. The Meat would be stopped.

****

Protocols existed for every contingency, hundreds of thousands of scenarios and situations which had never occurred had nonetheless been modeled and analyzed, extrapolated and resolved. If the Gardener felt any distress, it was less about its situation than the peculiarity of finding itself utilizing such procedures.

Complexities of redundancies defined its people's life view. What point even conceptualizing a venture if one were to begin without all possibilities accounted for? Viewed in such a light, its current predicament was at worst a minor inconvenience.

The initial seeding required only a two-percent success rate. Given sufficient time, even the most arid or acidic environment would yield success. But Meat, regardless of its manifestation, was always short-lived, which in turn meant that time was a limited resource. Fortunately, there was evidence of spillage around the target cargo container to suggest they contained a variety of organic matter, and in such profusion that inspection had resulted in a sample of the cargo escaping. The Gardener's released seeds absorbed the bits of debris and pursued the genetic option that it had activated in them before their dispersal.

Seven purge agents—the same tools it had lately planted by the tens of thousands on its garden world—took form and together advanced on the nearest container, working in concert along an accessible seam. Two pressed immature forward tendrils into that seam, even as the other five dedicated their brief existence to generating and transferring the powerful acids that allowed the initial pair to create microscopic runnels adequate for their pollen, which continued the process. These five withered, but had served their purpose. Complex carbon chains were altered, co-opted, shattered. Cracks radiated from several places along the seam, and just that simply, the two surviving purge agents breached the cargo container. The entire process had taken scant minutes.

The pair hefted the now-desiccated remnants of the other five purge agents that had already gone to seed and tore them into smaller bits, stuffing the pieces through the cracks into the organic matter below, grain of some form, more than adequate for the current need. These seeds fed upon the grain, broke it down, produced a new generation of seeds that in turn consumed still more grain and germinated into more purge agents, hundreds of them. They tore the cargo container apart from the inside. Half moved toward structures that the Meat had erected for their own inscrutable but offensive purposes. The remainder split into smaller groups, each targeting other standalone containers and, further afield, whole stacks of containers, to repeat their genesis. Soon, thousands of leafy agents advanced on the structures, tearing them open. Some entered to attack their contents—absorbing any organics and destroying inorganics, according to their genetics directives—others applied their talents to breaking down the Meat's structures themselves, guided by the directives the Gardener had built into their every fiber.

From the shattered safety of its pod, half-buried in mud and dirt, the Gardener directed its agents with a light touch, the majority of its focus devoted to ratiocination and the need to incorporate so much novel data into a plan to alert its people.

It scarcely noted when the remnants of its vessel arrived, delivered like plucked weeds and shattered branches to the far side of the array of cargo containers. In the fullness of time it would grow a new vessel, but that was a future concern and not something it allowed to intrude on its thoughts. Eventually, a more insistent interruption broke its concentration. Several squadrons of Mechs arrived, pulling its focus to their actions as they spawned confusion. With brutal efficiency the Mechs began destroying its purge agents with energy waves. But no, not actual Mech life, these nuisances were more

Meat, Meat that had developed technology to mimic the appearance and behavior of Mech. Their presence dictated a more nuanced response than it had built into the genes of its purge agents.

The Gardener had itself changed since arriving upon this world. Even as its agents had begun their work, a dedicated few had returned to it and sacrificed their newly grown bodies, supplying it with more base material. It had built up the ambulatory ganglia that supported its cranium, even as it had expanded the volume of its brain case and coaxed its cortex to expand to fill it, growing its cognitive abilities. As the tech-wearing Meat attacked, it spun off a trio of strategies, any one of which might resolve the conflict at hand.

From its pod's remaining seed bank, it jettisoned a precious few mega seeds, the advanced form of the utilitarian purge agents that could combine and grow to gargantuan proportions for those tasks that required macro rather than micro scales of action.

Next it unleashed a burst of anaerobic symbiotes. A fraction landed upon some of its purge agents and took over a portion of their surface area to generate aerodynamic pollens too small to be seen. These in turn wafted toward the Meat.

And finally, it reached into the dormant communication network that bound its purge agents, taking direct command of the different contingents of them to use them more strategically against the Meat foe.

Such an approach, hasty and multiplicitous, violated the Gardener's training and experience. When designing a world, it would expend vast time determining the one best and true way to accomplish its goal. But contingencies had forced it to invoke other methods. Any one strategy might be required, or two, perhaps all three. But when it was done, the Meat would be destroyed and there would be sufficient resources left for it to select a more purposeful course of action, alert its people to this new danger, and put end to the threat of the Meat.

☐

Part III: Seeds of Doubt

Colby lay in the darkness, his fingertips intertwined in Duke's fur—the only sensory input he had. The last of his plant hosts had been cut off five, ten, fifteen minutes ago. With only his thoughts, it was hard to keep track. It occurred to him that the Marines might opt to destroy the broken ship he arrived in, weighing the advantage gained by eliminating an unknown threat over the loss of alien technology. That possibility slowly grew, like a loose thread unraveling on a sweater, until it came to the fore and took over most of his thoughts. He needed to communicate, to let them know he was in here. But nothing he tried had yet allowed him to contact the Marines, and the troubleshooting worm he'd initiated during the fight had revealed nothing. It should have been simple. His implant should have inserted itself effortlessly into the comms net, but when he reached for the system—and he'd used the comm system on New Mars tens of thousands of times— it was as if nothing was there.

He'd been locked out, and it didn't take much effort to guess who had done it. Vice-

Minister Greenstein. The asshole, probably fearing that Colby would have started a rebellion when he was relieved of command, had blocked his implant from the tactical net.

The tiniest of vibrations reached him, pulling his attention away from all competing thoughts. Had it had been real or just his imagination? Then, a few moments later, he felt it again. What did it represent? Was the ship taking off, ready to be shot down, or were the Marines boarding it? Were more of the plant soldiers being harvested inside the ship? Colby didn't know enough to hazard a guess.

"It's OK, Duke," he whispered.

And then, like water in the desert, oh so faintly, he heard voices—human voices.

"In here!" he shouted, "In here!" as Duke let out a half-whine, half howl. The talking outside stopped, and he shouted out again, "I'm in here! In the wall!"

Nothing happened for a long minute. His mind swam with images of Marines firing their weapons into the ship's locker, prompting him to keep up a steady stream of pleas to help him.

Light cut the darkness of the locker. Colby squinted, eyes tearing with pain, but nonetheless tried to tilt his head up to see, but the vines crisscrossed his face, leaving only tiny gaps to see through. A Marine peered in, M86 pointed at him.

"What the fuck?" the Marine said.

"I'm Lieutenant General Colby Edson, Marines. Get me out of here!"

The Marine leaned back, passing out of Colby's view, and he said, "Sergeant, you're not going to believe this."

Colby felt a tap on the bottom of his foot, as if poked with the barrel of an M86. A man-packed version of the larger M88, it still fired the same rounds, any of which would be more than enough to end Colby's journey through life.

He caught a glimpse of a second figure. Keeping his voice calm with a huge force of will, he said, "Listen, Sergeant. I'm Lieutenant General Colby Edson, Republic Marines. I need you to get me out of here. I've got vital intel that has to be passed to higher headquarters."

"We don't got no General Edson on New Mars," the sergeant said, distrust plain in his voice.

"I'm retired now. But I'm still a Marine."

Duke chose that moment to whine, and the sergeant jumped back out of view.

"He's got a dog in there with him," someone said.

Colby didn't know if it was Duke or him that convinced the sergeant, but he said, "I'm sending a runner to get the lieutenant, sir. You hang on."

He didn't want to hang on, he wanted to be free. He was tired and hungry and had to get word to someone in charge because it was damn sure that Greenstein hadn't shared the report he'd sent before entering the wormhole. And to top it off, something about the light or maybe his interaction with the Marines was causing the vines to constrict even more. Colby recognized the early warning signs of a panic attack. He had to get out of the locker and out of the grasp of the ship.

"What's your name, Sergeant?"

"Sergeant Prius Mannigan, sir."

"Sergeant Mannigan, I've got to get out of here now. While we're waiting for your lieutenant, can you try and get me out of here?"

The sergeant hesitated, then asked, "What happens if I touch that stuff?"

"I. . . I don't know," he said, suddenly ashamed that he hadn't considered the question before asking. He didn't want to put the sergeant at risk. "Better not touch it, but if you've got a blade, maybe you can try to cut me loose?"

Asking a Marine if they had a blade was like asking them if they breathed.

"Corporal Lin, cover me," the sergeant said to someone out of Colby's sight. "I'm going to try and cut the general out."

The sergeant leaned forward, and a moment later, a searing pain shot up his leg. He screamed and Duke howled.

"Stop, stop!"

"I didn't cut you, sir. I know I didn't," the panicky-sounding sergeant shouted.

"Just don't do it again," Colby snapped, as waves of pain washed through him for a few moments before it diminished to more of an ache. "Let me think."

20/20 hindsight assured him that the vines hadn't just connected him to the plant soldiers, they'd bonded to him as well. He had to figure out a solution that didn't harm the vines. There was no way he'd survive being cut out.

"What's going on, Sergeant Mannigan?" a woman's voice reached him.

"There's some general in there, ma'am."

"And a dog," another voice added.

A new Marine took up position beside the sergeant and peered in. "Who are you, and what the hell are you doing in an enemy ship?"

"I'm Lieutenant General Colby Edson, Republic Marines. How I got here is a long story, and I'd prefer to only tell it once. Who's your commanding officer, Lieutenant?"

Only silence answered him. Colby had run out of patience. He snapped, "I'm not a fucking plant-soldier, in case you haven't noticed!"

"He looks like one, all trussed up like that," someone muttered from beyond his limited line-of-sight.

There was another long pause, then, "Captain Sotherby."

"Your commanding officer, not company commander," he said, struggling to hold back from erupting again. He might be a retired Marine Corps general, but he was trussed up like a New Year's hog on the spit, and this lieutenant had a platoon of armed Marines out there.

"Lieutenant Colonel Manuel Sifuentes, sir," she said grudgingly.

"Manny? Manny Sif?" Colby could have wept with relief. "Get word up to him. Tell him that I know what he did on Harris Reef!"

"Sir?"

"Just tell him who I am, and mention that I know about Harris Reef."

Manuel Sifuentes, of all people. "Manny Sif" had been a company commander for him, back when he was a colonel and the commanding officer of Marine Deployed Reaction Force 33. While at Harris Reef on a liberty call, the young captain. . . well, suffice it to say that events unfolded so that the captain had shown up stark naked at the liberty shuttle, begging the Navy chief for a ride back up to the ship. Colby had listened to the captain's story of woe, took pity on him, and decided that he'd been more of an innocent—well, not completely innocent—victim than a transgressor. He'd covered up for Manny Sif, ensuring nothing official was entered on his record.

The Marines outside the locker spoke in low tones while Colby lay there. At one point, someone muttered, "Just burn the suckers. They'll let go then."

"No one do anything until your CO gets here!" Colby shouted out. The Marines fell silent after that.

It took at least fifteen minutes before Colby heard activity outside. A familiar voice said, "So, just what is going on in this thing?"

Colby could see the lieutenant step back, and a moment later, an older-looking, but still recognizable, Manuel Sifuentes came into his view.

"Who are you?"

"Colby Edson, Manny." The colonel frowned and pulled back just a hair. "MADREF Thirty-Three, Harris Reef, a certain captain and a local young . . ."

"Shit! General Edson! You were shit-ca. . . you retired and went off to be a farmer somewhere. What the hell are you doing here?"

"Yes, I was shit-canned. And I was a farmer on Vasquez, and that's where the boss plant first invaded. I fought them off and took its ship, but as you can see, things kinda went to hell, and I'm stuck in here."

"These aliens attacked Vasquez? Why didn't we hear about that before they landed here?"

"I sent a report up, to Vice-Minister Greenstein."

"Nothing was promulgated. They surprised the shit out of us when they landed. What the hell are they, anyway?"

"I've got some ideas," Colby said, and I need to brief the staff. Who's the CG?"

"Brigadier General U Te, sir."

Well, it could be worse. She was a bit of a brown-noser when she was a battalion commander, but she should listen to reason.

Despite the importance of New Mars, despite the presence of a Marine Sector command, the planet only had a reinforced Marine battalion and the local militia for defense. The civilian officials on New Mars liked having the generals with them, but they feared combat troops that could theoretically take charge, though nothing like that had happened for over four hundred years. But as a result, the Marines were limited to a single combat battalion. That battalion was part of Ninth Division, but the bulk of the division was based on Mongut III, two wormhole jumps away.

"I really need to brief her and her staff, but I can't do it like this. You've got to get me out of here."

"We tried to cut him out, sir, but he screamed as soon as we cut the vines," the sergeant said.

"And the dog cried, too," another voice called out.

"Manny. . . uh, Colonel," he said, "I'm somehow connected to this thing. I feel what's happening to it."

"Are you still, you know. . . are you still, you, sir?" the lieutenant colonel asked, leaning his head into the locker and speaking too softly for his men to hear.

"Yes, I'm still me," Colby said.

I hope I'm still me.

"Sir, Master Sergeant Jelavić comes from a farming family. Maybe he can figure something out?" the lieutenant said.

"Well, hell, it can't hurt to see if he's got any ideas. Good thinking, Lieutenant. Someone get him over here.

"How the hell did they shut down our battlesuits, General?' he asked Colby, turning back to him. "We're down to 17 percent effective. Do you know how they managed that?"

Colby didn't know, but the image of the green mist of atomized plant bodies came unbidden to his mind. Something told him the mist was part of that.

Before he could articulate even that vague thought, Sifuentes held up a hand to silence him with the familiar look of someone listening to an implant.

"Major Lyme, did you get that?" he yelled out to someone out of sight, probably his XO or operations officer. "OK, get the company commanders ready. We need to move. All of you inside this ship, get to your companies now!"

"Manny! What's going on?"

"Sorry, General, you're going to have to stay put for now. I'll send someone back for you when I can."

"Why? What's happening?"

"One of your plants broke into the food containers and is growing out-of-control. We've got to stop it before it gets God knows how big!"

****

Colby was going batshit crazy. He had light now, at least, but he still couldn't move. Wiggling his fingers and toes just didn't count. Duke clearly felt the same way; since the Marines had left she hadn't stopped whining and nothing he could say calmed her. Her discomfort only fueled his own frustration. Manny Sif could have left at least one

Marine with him, maybe that farmer master sergeant who could figure out how to free him.

Then he felt a little guilty for feeling put out. Colby had seen the giant plant warriors back on Vasquez. They'd been like some vegetable version of the daikaiju from the Hollybolly remakes of ancient B-movies. And like those movie monsters, these plants had been powerful enough to tear apart a massive launch cannon and they looked pretty unstoppable. With a full Marine division and a couple of cruisers, they'd make short work of the plants, but he wasn't sure how a reinforced battalion, especially one down to 17 percent battlesuits, would fare. He wished he could be out there with them. It hurt to know Marines were marching to danger while he lay there like a piece of cargo. He had to get out of the ship to help in any way he could.

"Hell, Duke. I guess it's up to us, huh girl?"

He'd already tried to push his consciousness to whatever was out there growing, hoping that he could somehow affect it. But there was nothing. When he reached out as he had with the plant soldier he couldn't find anything to connect to. It was as if he was lost in a sea of black cotton that held him tight inside his green prison. Everything beyond the ship's hull was an empty void. At least inside, he had some input. If he looked down, he could see the lump of vines that was Duke, and straight ahead he could see a narrow sector of the ship's bridge. It wasn't much, but it was so much better than the blackness he'd endured before. Without that little bit of light he would be crazy, and probably wondering if Manny and the other Marines had just been a fevered dream.

Inside the ship? I can't sense anything outside, but I can see inside, and what is this thing but just another plant?

He felt a slight jolt of excitement. He'd felt pain when the vines holding him had been cut, which meant they were connected. All he had to do was figure out a way to open than connection, and then maybe he could get the vines to release him.

"But how the hell do I do that?" he said aloud, reverting to his habit of talking things through. "OK, think of it like an enemy comms network, shielded from eavesdropping. How do we break into that? Standard operating procedure would be to use either subterfuge, worm my way in, or a resort to a brute force attack."

Colby had enough respect for the boffins he'd met over the course of his military career to know he didn't have the brain power to hack into a system even if he had a controllable interface. But he did have his implant, and that gave him some pretty impressive power options. It took him a good ten minutes to go through the mental gymnastics required to set up what he wanted. He ran a quick self-check, and it looked like it would work. Maybe.

He hesitated a second before starting it. There was no way to know how the ship would react. It could recognize the attack for what it was and take action to eliminate the source. Colby didn't think getting strangled by vines would be a particularly comfortable way to go. But that was a chance he had to take. Visualizing a big red button, he mentally pressed it.

He didn't feel any different, yet he knew the implant was sending thousands of thrusts at the ship, trying to find a crack in the alien operating system and forcing it wider. Colby tried to focus, ordering the vines to release them, pushing against nothing in hopes that his implant could open, identify, and exploit even the tiniest of portals. It was difficult, though, with Duke whining, but there was nothing he could do about that. The poor dog had reached her limit.

Twice, the vines jerked, giving his heart a jolt as he pictured squeezing the life out of them, but his attempts to control them got nowhere. He was beginning to feel the futility of it all when suddenly, as if picked up by a tsunami, he was carried. . . somewhere? He was inside the ship. Not like his body was inside the locker, but more intimately within the core of it.

Stop! he ordered his implant.

Odd sensations streamed into him, some hybrid of the connection provided by the vines and the efforts of his implant. He reached out tentatively, trying to figure out just what/where he was, trying and rejecting analogies and metaphors until he found one that fit. As best as he could comprehend it he was almost an extension of the ship—or it was an extension of him. He couldn't tell. He focused on the vines, and ordered them to release him. Nothing happened. He could see them, he could almost feel them as they held Duke and him fast, but they wouldn't respond to his commands. Unlike the soldiers, it was as if they couldn't understand what he was ordering them to do.

"Hell, I'm being undone by the stupid ones," he said.

He cast around the ship, hoping there were any mobile plants left. He'd seen plenty of them back on Vasquez, taking readings and scuttling about on plant tasks that looked to have more to do with fieldwork than invasion. It was then he realized that, other than the boss plant, he hadn't seen any mobile plants since he'd been aboard.

"They've got to be somewhere."

Colby started projecting himself through the ship, taking a virtual tour. . . except, it wasn't virtual. Part of him was actually traveling around the broken ship, noting the damage done by the cargo drone and poking into every compartment. Meanwhile, the rest of him was stuck inside the locker. It felt different than when he was controlling the soldier plants.

He didn't find any of the little, diagnostic plants hiding out, nor anything he could use to free himself. He found one compartment that reeked of potential, if that made sense. Literally, it was as if something pinged his brain about unnamed possibilities when he focused his awareness on that tiny section. But there was nothing there over which he could take control.

When the first search turned up empty, he did it again. Still nada. The only thing that tickled his senses was the small compartment that felt like potential. And then it clicked.

"Seeds!" he said. "They've got to be seeds! What else defines potential for a plant? If I can—" But the ramifications and his own reservations halted his words.

Somewhere outside the ship, Marines were in battle with giant plants. Those plant warriors, not the smaller soldiers, were the problem, not the solution. More of them would only add more to the mess.

Or would they? I could control the other soldiers. What if I can sprout new ones and then use them to fight?

He didn't consider how long it would take to grow new fighters to soldier-size. On Vasquez, it had taken over a day, but if he understood what Manny Sif had said, the daikaiju were growing at an exponential rate. Maybe he could get these to grow that fast, too. A little of Señor Fukimaru's Wonder Grow went a long way back on his farm to increase yield, and there had to be an equivalent here on the ship that could do the same thing.

You might have been a Marine general, but you've been a farmer for the last two years, for goodness' sake. Just figure it out, Edson!

Before he consciously decided to actually germinate the seeds, his mind was questing inside the compartment, and almost immediately, he recognized what had to be a nutrient feed system. He hesitated for only a moment before he tried to trip it. He might not have been able to control the vines holding him, but to his welcome surprise, the nutrient broth started to flow into the mass of seeds.

Almost immediately, the seeds, well, stirred, as if waking up. He nervously monitored them, hoping he hadn't a mistake. He might be compounding his initial sin of letting the plants onto New Mars.

Within a minute, the seeds began to sprout, tiny green tendrils reaching out. Colby tried to reach them, but other than an itch in his mind that he couldn't scratch, he didn't feel a connection.

Maybe they don't have a developed enough whatever-they-had-for-a-brain yet.

There had to be thousands of the seeds. As the green tendrils grew larger, longer, the new sprouts used them to start pulling themselves out of their separate bins and onto the deck. Within five minutes, five-centimeter-tall "starts," to use farming terminology, were crawling out of the compartment and invading the rest of the ship.

Colby couldn't see any of them yet. His very limited field of vision was a little above waist height and only with a few degrees of arc. He wasn't sure, for that matter, just how he was "seeing" any of this. He knew it was through the ship itself somehow, but he didn't have a clue how that worked. But he could see it, and that was all that mattered for now.

More of the starts poured out of the compartment. To Colby's surprise, two of the immature plants started to bond to each other. For a moment it seemed they were fighting, like fetal sharks inside their mother's womb, but then they merged, forming a single, larger plant. The newly formed double plant then sought two more merged plants, and within a minute, had combined into a single, still larger plant.

The top of something green passed into Colby's vision for a second and then was gone. A moment later, another appeared as the plants—he couldn't call them starts any longer—continued their combinatorial dance.

Two leafy arms reached up into the locker, gained purchase and pulled the body of a plant up to join him.

"Stop, stop!" he yelled, focusing his effort.

The plant barely hesitated. It pulled itself further into the locker, climbing the wall somehow, not touching him yet. Another followed it, then a third. Duke started snarling, but the plant paid no attention to the dog. Colby attempted to struggle, remembering how his neighbors, the Gustavsons, had been killed by the plant soldiers, how they had attacked him on the farm and in Blair de Staffney Station. He didn't want to die trussed up like this. Striving to remain calm, he sent out waves of orders for the plants to leave the locker. He could feel them, better than when they were sprouts and starts, but he still couldn't control them.

The first plant reached out to touch one of the vines holding his leg. That vine went limp, almost swooned. It released Colby and started to merge with the larger plant. Other plants reached in, tendrils questing one by one for the vines that imprisoned him, and those vines released him as well. When one of the plants encircled his leg with a supple branch of an arm, Colby tried to jerk back, afraid that somehow, he'd be absorbed, too, but as if tasting him and finding him unworthy, the arm jerked back.

The locker filled with writhing plants, their number decreasing as they grew from absorbing vine after vine. Duke started barking and wriggling beside him as each gripping vine let go in turn. Colby felt a final vine across his chest fall away. He sat up, pushing at the plants in his excitement to be free. With no more vines, they slid out of the locker, presumably to seek more fodder for mergers.

Duke didn't care why they were gone—she bolted from the locker with a yelp and out into the mass of smaller plants on the deck of the ship. She started jumping and spinning, crashing into them as she exulted in being free. The plants she knocked over ignored her antics and simply picked themselves back up. They looked identical to the ones that had invaded Vasquez, but they acted in a different manner.

Colby had been filling in a picture of the alien species, and he was pretty sure that the boss plant controlled the others. If so, then was it possible that they had to be programmed or ordered to attack humans? Which meant that these plants, of which the boss had no knowledge, hadn't received such orders yet. Did that mean he had an opportunity to program them? The larger they got, the more Colby began experiencing whispers of plant-thought, as if their brains were only now beginning to reach some critical mass needed to be controlled.

But that still left the question of the plant boss. Colby had no doubt that cabbage-head was alive and out there, controlling whatever giant plant warriors were now attacking the Marines. Would the boss show up here and take over these plants? Colby vowed not to let that happen. Now he just had to figure out how to back up promises with deeds.

Before he could do that, though, he had to get out of the ship. More than a dozen of the plants had grown to his chest-level in height. A few seemed to be merging with the ship itself. He'd been able to control the plant soldiers when they were attacking the factory outside while he was trapped in the ship, then by the symmetric property of equality, he should be able to control those on the ship from outside of it.

This wasn't algebra, he knew, but he really had to get off the ship. Claustrophobia had him on the edge of a panic attack that he couldn't currently afford.

"Duke! Let's go, girl," he shouted.

She barked what he assumed to be her assent. He started pushing his way through the unresisting plants towards the ship's hatch, she darted under them, weaving her way between their stalks.

The aft end of the ship had been heavily damaged by the cargo drone's arms, and the ship had created temporary patches to stop the flow of air even after Colby had climbed into the locker. He hadn't seen them before, more worried about breathing than in admiring a feat of biological engineering. As he watched, the obvious patches were fading. All around him plants were reaching up and being absorbed into the bulkhead, like so much vegetable wall putty.

"Shit!" he said, wondering what was happening to the hatch itself. It had been a tight fit before just to get through it into the ship—he hoped it was still there. He couldn't see it through the mob of plants pressing themselves against that part of the wall. He couldn't even see Duke any more, and only knew her location when he she gave another yelp. Plants flew left and right and as Colby ducked down, he could see his dog shoving plants out of her way as she pushed her way to the open hatch. His heart dropped as he saw it already closing.

"Wait, Duke!" he shouted, scrabbling forward on his hands and knees, but Duke, seeing sunshine, was not waiting for anything.

She darted ahead and through the opening. Her passage through spurred the sphincter-like hatch to begin closing faster. With a burst of speed, Colby darted forward, following Duke's example and sending plants flying. He could see the dog on the outside as she stopped and looked back at him, barking furiously.

"I'm coming, girl!" he shouted, crawling as fast as he could, but in the best Hollybolly tradition, the opening kept shrinking, and in this case the hero didn't make it. By the time he reached it, the opening wouldn't have even accommodated a child. He stuck his hand through the hole, desperate to force it back open, but he couldn't even slow it down. Duke licked his hand before he had to jerk it back for fear of being trapped—or worse, losing his arm.

"Son-of-a-bitch!" he yelled in frustration, kicking out and scattering more of the smaller plants.

Even among the plants from which he had torn limbs, they all ignored him. But that didn't mean they wouldn't notice him if he started taking them all on. He leaned back against the bulkhead, letting his emotions drain away until his mind felt numb.

Only, it wasn't really numb. There was an incessant buzzing that he'd at first thought an actual sound before realizing his ears weren't hearing any of it. He opened his mind, staring at one of the merged plants, this one about a meter-and-a-half tall. He imagined himself enveloping it, as he had with the plant soldiers in the factory, and he told it to stop.

It did.

Evidently, the plants had to grow large enough, or merge with enough others before their neural network could pick up commands.

"Open the hatch!" he ordered it.

Just as with the plant soldiers, he doubted they understood his words per se, responding instead to the underlying intention. Whatever the mechanism, the plant moved to the correct spot along the bulkhead and pressed up against it.

And, of course, given his luck, nothing happened. The hatch did not reappear, and the bulkhead remained as featureless as before. Colby left the plant mindlessly striving to open a hole in the hull of the ship and shifted his attention deeper into the ship itself. He was just as attuned to the vessel as the individual plants, but he couldn't control it. He could sense the capability just out of reach, but even with his interface, he lacked some critical piece that would allow him that connection.

He could feel the ship growing all around him, changing in response to the plants he'd unleashed from seeds. More and more plants melded into the walls of the ship, emerging and continuing to grow on the outside, branches extending across the ground in all directions even as it enveloped the ship itself in ropy vines reminiscent of the ones that had held him prisoner. Following some blueprint he couldn't fathom the ship began to transform. Finally only a few plants remained inside the ship's compartment and these spaced themselves at even intervals from one another and began to sprout heavy branches, filling up more and more of the available space.

The process wasn't entirely comfortable. Colby felt as if he had gas, his stomach spasming as he explored the ship through his connection. It seemed as if the ship was no longer the central entity, as if the plants kept merging into a larger and larger form, one that had opted to incorporate the ship into itself. Somewhere in the process it had stopped being a ship that he was using to grow plants in.

If it isn't the ship, but another plant, can I control that?

He reached out, the connection familiar and different but tenuous, like trying to understand Italian when all you spoke was Spanish. Before he could try to exert control, the ship lurched, throwing Colby backwards across the deck.

Those branches were legs! This thing has become one of the giant plant monsters!

Colby reached out to the plant itself, ignoring the capsule that was the ship, and he let his awareness flow into it. There was no disorientation as there had initially been with the plant soldiers. This was even more familiar than slipping into an old pair of shoes that knew his feet from long use. He'd done this a thousand times before, in a Republic Marine Corps battlesuit. It didn't matter if a giant plant was really the same, or if his implant was translating the process into something his mind could comprehend. Those kinds of questions could wait until later. What mattered now was that he felt more in control than he'd been since leaving Vasquez. A few tentative impulses flickered over him, expressing a vague concern, or possibly opposition from the plant warrior around him, but it took no effort for Colby to squash them.

With a simple mental flick, he was aware of what was outside of him. He was aware of a small golden dog biting a tiny corner of his leg. He was aware of combat in the distance, of Marines, almost all on foot, being attacked by thousands of suicidal plant soldiers. He was aware of three more giants much larger than the pair that had torn apart the launch cannon back on Vasquez. These plant warriors ignored the puny attempts by humans to stop them as they destroyed what he recognized as the governmental administration complex.

"Sorry Duke," he said as he stepped forward, careful not to accidentally fling the tiny dog aside. "Looks like I'm getting into the shit after all."

****

Like a Norse Jötunn emerging from the earth, Colby stood up, towering over the shattered factories and cargo containers. It should have felt odd, but it didn't. Perspective aside, the metaphor held. This was no different than donning a battlesuit. Muscle and nervous memory took over, and he strode forward. He didn't have to "think" each tree-like leg in turn, no more so than he would to take a normal stroll—he wanted to move forward, and the legs took over.

Despite his ability to control the giant plant, he had not been absorbed into it. He may have expanded his sense of self, but the core of who he was resided in the human body that slumped on the deck of what had been the alien ship. That body rolled at each lurching step. Much more of that and he'd awaken to a mass of bruises when all was done. He sent out a tentative command,

and this time, the bulkheads of the ship obeyed, sending out several tendrils that delicately wrapped around his body, like the harness inside a battlesuit. With his physical body secure, he turned his attention back to the outside world. The process had taken only seconds.

There were small eddies of green mist dotting the ground, like puddles after a rain. They stirred as he stepped into them, rising in swirls around his legs, attaching thousands of tiny potential-plants to him. He could feel the life force they contained, life force that translated into brute power. Colby knew without knowing how that it was power he could tap.

His perception of distance skewed as he settled into his new height. Up ahead he could see the tops of three giant plants—daikaiju, he thought, recalling the term once more. They rampaged in what he knew to be Christiaan Huygens City, the capital of the planet. He didn't have to see them, though, to know where to go. He could feel them, their presence shined like a beacon in his mind, the distance to them defined in terms of the number of strides he'd need to reach them. It didn't have to make sense, it just was.

Reflexes honed by endless hours in a battlesuit had him reaching through his implant to call up a targeting routine with the intention of painting the three giants and assigning a series of missiles to each once he locked on. His implant pinged back empty, unable to mesh with the software or access the requested armament because of course he wasn't actually in his familiar battlesuit. The analogy only went so far. Colby would have to carry the battle to his foe the old fashioned way. Still, missiles would have been nice.

He crushed immobile battlesuits as he strode along. He wasn't trying to stomp on them, but there wasn't much open space to place his huge feet, not if he wanted to take the most direct route and reach the fight ahead. He could sense firing, he could sense the battle, but couldn't hear the sounds of the conflict. He briefly wondered if the plants even had hearing in the way that humans did. It didn't matter. Whatever sensory capability came with his daikaiju was more than adequate to understand what was going on.

With his mind wandering as to whether he could hear or not, he almost crushed a pocket of a dozen Marines who were being attacked by smaller plant soldiers. The Marines turned to face him, firing their puny weapons which were about as annoying as gnats to him—less annoying, in fact. Colby paused for a moment, taking the time to sweep a huge hand through the attacking plant soldiers, knocking them down like ten-pins. He grasped a handful as he resumed walking and tried to push them into his thigh, to absorb them. It didn't work, so he let the mangled bodies fall to the ground as they released more spores.

The fighting ahead was getting heavier, and Colby tried to break into a run. The result was almost comical. He stumbled, almost fell, as he became aware that he possessed a multitude of arms because he windmilled them wildly to keep his balance. Whatever else the daikaiju were, they were not built to be runners. He went back to walking, marginally increased his speed, and had to be satisfied with that.

His sense of time had turned fuzzy as well. In something more than five minutes but less than ten, he entered the city. Marines in battlesuits were attacking the three daikaiju with heavy weapons, but their massive bodies seemed to simply absorb what was fired at them. Which isn't to say they didn't notice. One of the three picked up a huge chunk of what had been part of the planetary administrative building and flung it at the Marines. Several battle-suited Marines were knocked out of the fight.

As he approached, some of the remaining Marines fired at him. Their missiles and heavy rounds were beyond gnat-annoying, but not by much. Colby would rather they not fire at him, but he could bear it. Nukes might be another matter.

He knew the militia had them, but as long as the city still functioned, and as long as there were humans still alive in it, he doubted the clearance to deploy them would be given. Which was just as well—he didn't want to test his new body against that kind of destructive power.

Not my new body, he told himself. I'm still me. This is just a huge, organic battlesuit.

He wasn't quite sure what he was going to do as he strode down Morrison Way and approached the administration building. There were three giant plant warriors there working their way through the huge building. It wasn't until he entered the square, where the Victory Fountain lay in rubble, water shooting into the air, that he realized he was looking down at the other three. He didn't tower over them, but he was taller. Looking down at the branches that served as arms, he realized that he out-massed them, too. Together, they were three to his one, so combined, they out-massed him, but he was larger—and hopefully more powerful—than any single one of them.

A missile streaked out and hit Colby low in his torso.

Hell, guys! Stop it! he thought, turning around to face them.

He didn't have any vocal chords, nor any way to make a sound, however. He swung his many arms as if waving off a troop carrier landing, but far from communicating his desires it just triggered two more missiles. There wasn't much he could do about them, and it was only an annoyance—even if they did hurt—so he swung back to the other three diakaiju.

As if sensing him, two of them parted a few steps, giving him room to join in the mayhem. He took advantage of that, getting closer before he sent out a focused metal command for the one on his left to stop.

It didn't.

He tried again, but the giant plant didn't even hesitate. Colby didn't think he'd even penetrated the giant—it was as if there was something blocking him, like a shield. It was as if they were on different frequencies—or something more powerful was in control.

Where is the boss plant? Colby asked himself, turning around to scan the city. Was it aware that he'd taken control of some of its plant soldiers earlier, and had it found a way to block him?

He didn't expect to actually see it, Life had never come at him so easily. Besides, the damn thing could be anywhere. But on the off chance that it was there and within range of being crushed by a well-placed massive foot he'd had to look.

There was nothing left for him to do. With a mental sigh, he reached from behind the nearest giant and wrapped it up with his arms. When he had it thoroughly entwined in his grip, Colby lifted it off its feet. The giant squirmed in his grasp. It was ungodly strong, but Colby was stronger, and without its feet to brace it, it had no leverage. It grasped at him, pulling, desperate to grapple. Colby lost a few minor arms in the attempt. He braced himself, expecting to go into shock as he felt limbs being torn from his body, but his connection ignored that—too human—reaction. After all, it wasn't like he didn't have plenty of limbs to spare, so the loss of a few was really inconsequential.

The realization was both disconcerting and liberating. He shifted the daikaiju in his grip, and began swinging it like a baseball bat, beating it against the side of the half-demolished building. Bits of marble, granite, and plasticrete broke off— along with larger bits of green plant matter. Chunks of plant flew in all directions as Colby swung again and again, effectively smashing the plant to bits. Still, the arms grabbed at him, even when half of the plant was spread all over the building and into the square. He kept swinging and only stopped when his opponent finally went limp.

He dropped the broken remnants and turned to face the other two, who had paused in their own rampage. They didn't have eyes, but there was no doubt that they were "looking at him."

Getting orders from above, huh?

As one, they moved forward to engage him, and Colby stepped back into the square. He might be bigger than either of them, but two-to-one were not great odds. He needed room to maneuver. If they managed to close with him together he wouldn't stand a chance.

As he backed away one thing immediately registered. They bumped each other in their single-minded determination to rend him into his own green mist. They shared an objective but were not working as a team, and that sparked the beginnings of a plan. Two could defeat one as a team in almost every situation but only when working in tandem. A savvy fighter could turn their inability to work as a team into an advantage.

Colby was a savvy fighter, courtesy of the Marine Corps Martial Arts Program. All those hours of pain, all those hours where Master Sergeant Burke Dorcas tortured him within a centimeter of his life, came flooding back to him. All those bouts fighting two other Marines at the same time—which almost always ended up with him getting the shit kicked out of him—had imbedded muscle memory that took over, even after all these years, even applied to a giant plant body that he happened to be wearing.

He backed up, leading them out of the ruined building, and just as they reached what had once been the Grand Rotunda, he feinted to the right. Both of his opponents wheeled to cut him off, which was just what Colby wanted. He pivoted on one leg, delivering what had to be the most powerful spinning back kick in the history of the human race. It connected low on the closer giant, sending it backward into the second, tangling them both up for long enough for him to step in and deliver a stomp with all of the kilotons of force he could generate. A chunk of the nearer daikaiju turned into mush. Colby tried to take advantage of the situation to deliver another stomp, but this time, as his foot hit, the other plant warrior managed to snake an arm around its companion and snag Colby's foot as he tried to withdraw. He jerked back and almost toppled, hopping away. He couldn't afford a fall here; it would be a mortal error. It was only because the other two were tangled up together that he was able to retreat back into the square and stabilize himself.

By that time, the other two had untangled themselves and squared off against him again.

The first one leaked greenish fluid from two pulverized areas on its trunk. It was still in the fight however, showing no signs of distress as it advanced on Colby into the square.

There was a small explosion against one of the giant's crushed areas, as a Marine tried to take advantage of the situation. The wounded plant didn't flinch, and the Marine fire died off.

Colby had to keep maneuvering, he had to position the other two so they'd continue to get in each other's way. Most of all, he couldn't risk getting tangled up with both of them a second time. If he was caught, he was a dead man (plant).

He dredged up every single trick he remembered from his MCMAP training—and then added in some from pure street brawling for good measure. At one point, he ripped a cerrosteel support beam out of a ruined building and started swinging it around like a madman, raining blows on the other two, sending plant bits flying. It was gratifying but not all that effective, and it cost him an arm when he got too cocky and one of his opponents latched on and yanked back.

He darted in with kicks and blows, trying to hit and retreat before they could react. More often than not, his greatest opportunities came when the other two got in each other's way. The first one, the one he'd stomped, was slowly being broken, blow by blow. One leg, leaking a green ichor, buckled. Colby feinted, and the other tripped over its comrade in its eagerness to get at him. Colby had been waiting for this moment, and he grabbed the fifteen-meter-tall statue of Admiral of the Navy Fergusson Bianci, which had graced the square for centuries. He ripped it off its granite foundation, confident the admiral would approve of his plan. Spinning it around as if it were made of paper-mâché, he lunged forward and drove it into the base of what Colby thought of the giant's neck, pushing the admiral's upraised arm through the plant with enough momentum to both knock his foe over and drive the statue's arm into the ground.

It spasmed, reaching for the statue with a trio of limbs, but its power was gone. It wasn't dead, but it was out of the fight, for the time being at least.

The second giant closed with him before Colby could recover, but the time for running was over. Colby was hurt, missing minor arms and a chunk of one massive thigh, but so was the remaining giant. Now was the time to take on his opponent and let mass carry the day.

Mass nearly wasn't enough. Evidently, giant plant warriors had their own hand-to-hand combat techniques, and when they weren't getting into each other's way, these could be very effective indeed. They grappled like titans and crashed to the ground with a force that threatened to topple the surrounding buildings. Colby got on top of the other giant, which should have been a huge advantage but he somehow found himself slowly being crushed as a dozen arms wrapped around his torso and all but two of his own arms and grinding them to splinters. His connection flickered and he knew he didn't have long. With his remaining arms he grasped the other giant's nominal head and started pounding it into the stone slabs that made up the square. This was going to be a race to see who could remain conscious the longest. Colby sensed he had only seconds left when the other plant stopped applying pressure, its body limp. He'd won, but barely.

Never, ever underestimate your opponent, Edson!

He'd managed to take out the first daikaiju by using his brains and training, but assuming that might made right, he allowed the fight to be controlled by his opponent—that mistake almost cost him his life.

Colby got to his knees and slowly stood up. The plant beneath him was dead, green mist already forming. Behind him, the other giant was still alive weakly pulling at Admiral Bianci. There was no way he was going to give it a chance to recover. Crossing over to the impaled giant, Colby pushed one of his smaller hands into the creature's wound and imagined reaching through his fingers into fallen plant, questing for control. He'd been blocked before, but whether from the physical contact or its weakened state he felt a flicker of contact. Even as he tried to exploit it he could feel new walls being erected, batting aside his commands for the daikaiju to quit, give up, surrender.

Let's see how far we can push the whole battlesuit analogy.

He cleared his mind, imagined the heads up display of his battlesuit and pictured the emergency molt button. As he pressed it, he willed the logical sequence of events into his opponent. A sequence that, even if that damn boss plant cabbage head was calling the shots, it would never see coming.

With a spasmodic jerk the plant warrior went completely rigid. An instant later wisps of green mist drifted free from all over its body.

"Elvis has left the building," Colby said to himself. He was three-for-three and the enemy had been defeated. He let out a huge mental sigh. . . as a missile slammed into his gut.

Oh, come on, guys!

He already ached from his to-the-death wrestling match, and this missile hurt. He didn't know how many more he could absorb, but he certainly couldn't attack the Marines to get them to quit.

"C'mon, Edson, figure out how to show these people you're on their side before they bring out the big guns and you're taken down by friendly fire."

He was overthinking it, thinking, in fact, like a general. That was the problem; the Marines firing on him weren't generals. He had to give them something they'd understand, right down to the greenest private.

Only one thing fit the bill. Colby drew himself to his best drill field position of attention, held it for a count of five before he very deliberately moved into a position of parade rest, then froze. A few rounds hit him, then they petered out.

He waited like that, five, ten, who knows how many minutes. Finally, there was motion at the far end of the square. Thirty Marines appeared behind a mobile artillery piece, the 155 mm gun aimed right at him. He recognized one of the Marines, to his relief.

Slowly, so as not to startle the Marines into firing, he came back to a position of attention and using only a single arm rendered the best salute he could given he was working with a massive tree branch.

He couldn't hear anything, but he could sense Lieutenant Colonel Manuel Sifuentes ask, "General Edson?"

With as much grace as he could manage, Colby cut away the salute and nodded his giant, leafy head.

****

Colby took a sip of the coffee, savoring it. Duke lay on her back at his feet, sound asleep. He still hadn't processed what had happened—he was aware of everything, but he wasn't quite sure how to analyze things, and he couldn't bring himself to discuss things with Manny Sif. While only a lieutenant colonel, Manny was the de facto head of the government on New Mars, the second most important planet in human space.

The administrative building had been destroyed, and all the civilian staff as well as General U Te, had been killed in the attack. After Manny had sent a full report through the wormhole, the response from Earth had been brief and clear. He'd been ordered to implement martial law, with himself in charge, until someone could come to relieve him.

Colby had sent off his report as well, but he was glad that this time there was corroboration. A certain vice-minister couldn't accuse him of inventing an emergency as a way to worm himself back onto active duty.

The surviving Marines were congratulating themselves on their victory. At Colby's suggestion (retired, he couldn't give orders, only suggest, but taking out the trio of daikaiju had earned him their respect), they had burned the three giant and smaller soldier bodies. The regular soldiers had surprisingly collapsed when the giants had been defeated, and Manny Sif thought they were related.

Colby wasn't so sure. Maybe because he'd spent so much time connected to the plants, he was attuned to them. He could swear he'd felt another presence out there, operating beneath the level of his own connection. He was sure it was the boss plant. If he was right, then a far more likely explanation was that after losing the three giants, the plant boss had cut its losses and bugged out, all the better to prepare for another effort.

There certainly was enough raw material for another plant army. There hadn't been any way to collect up all the spores that had been released when the plants died. Manny Sif was sure they'd achieved victory, and Colby didn't think the brass back on Earth understood the gravity of the situation. From their perspective, a single battalion had defeated these aliens, so how could they be a threat to all of humanity?

A follow-up message from Earth included orders to seal off the wormhole to Vasquez, but that had to be put on hold, at least temporarily until a rescue party could go back and rescue Topeka and Riordan and anyone else who might have survived.

Colby saw no point in sealing off the wormhole after the rescue party returned. It would be like closing the barn door after the horses escaped. The plant boss was somewhere on New Mars, and it would be plotting—and maybe communicating with wherever its kind called home.

In a way, he felt sorry for it. He didn't want to admit it, but he'd been one of them, in a way. Maybe it was Stockholm Syndrome, or maybe he just had some deeper insight that had seeped into him, but all the death and destruction hadn't had a malevolent feel to it, any more than when he had dusted his crops on Vasquez for weeds. Was all the death and destruction just a terrible mistake? If they could just communicate, might it be possible to make peace with the plants?

Oh, come on, Edson. Next you'll be singing Kumbaya.

This wasn't over, not by a long shot, and the risk was still unimaginable.

At his feet, Duke whined, deep within a dog dream, one that Colby could guess.

"Yes, you know girl, don't you? We've got to find that boss plant."

END OF BOOK TWO

Thank you for reading *Scorched Earth*. We hope you enjoyed it. Book 3, with Colby and Duke continuing their fight against the Gardener, will be out soon. We welcome your review of our novella on Amazon or any other website.

SEEDS OF WAR
Invasion
Scorched Earth
Book 3 (Coming Soon).

Other Books by Lawrence M. Schoen

If you would like updates on Lawrence's new books releases, news, or special offers, please consider signing up for his mailing list. Your email will not be sold, rented, or in any other way disseminated. If you are interested, please sign up at the link below:

http://eepurl.com/c7257X

Barsk

Barsk: The Elephants' Graveyard
The Moons of Barsk

The Amazing Conroy
Buffalito Buffet
Calendrical Regression
Barry's Deal

Buffalito Destiny
Trial of the Century
Buffalito Contingency

Selected Short Stories

A Fool's Death
Bidding the Walrus
Pidgin
Mars Needs Baby Seals
The Game of Leaf and Smile
The Moment
Thinking
The Wrestler and the Spear Fisher

Books Edited/Published by Lawrence M. Schoen

Alembical
Alembical 2
Alembical 3
Cats in Space - Elektra Hammond (ed)
Cucurbital 2
Cucurbital 3
Eyes Like Sky and Coal and Moonligh - Cat Rambo
Rejiggering The Thingamajig And Other Stories - Eric James Stone
The Wizard of Macatawa and Other Stories - Tom Doyle

Other Books by Jonathan Brazee

If you would like updates on Jonathan's new books releases, news, or special offers, please consider signing up for his mailing list. Your email will not be sold, rented, or in any other way disseminated. If you are interested, please sign up at the link below:

http://eepurl.com/bnFSHH

The United Federation Marine Corps

Recruit
Sergeant
Lieutenant
Captain
Major
Lieutenant Colonel
Colonel
Commandant

Rebel
(Set in the UFMC universe.)

Behind Enemy Lines
(A UFMC Prequel)

The Accidental War (A Ryck Lysander Short Story
Published in *BOB's Bar: Tales from the Multiverse*)

The United Federation Marine Corps' Lysander Twins

Legacy Marines
Esther's Story: Recon Marine
Noah's Story: Marine Tanker
Esther's Story: Special Duty
Blood United

Coda

Women of the United Federation Marine Corps

Gladiator
Sniper
Corpsman

High Value Target (A Gracie Medicine Crow Short Story)
BOLO Mission (A Gracie Medicine Crow Short Story)
Weaponized Math (A Gracie Medicine Crow Novelette, First published in *The Expanding Universe 3*)

The United Federation Marine Corps' Grub Wars

Alliance
The Price of Honor
Division of Power

The Navy of Humankind: Wasp Squadron
Fire Ant
Crystals

Ghost Marines
Integration

The Return of the Marines Trilogy
The Few
The Proud
The Marines

The Al Anbar Chronicles: First Marine Expeditionary Force--Iraq
Prisoner of Fallujah
Combat Corpsman
Sniper

Werewolf of Marines
Werewolf of Marines: Semper Lycanus
Werewolf of Marines: Patria Lycanus
Werewolf of Marines: Pax Lycanus

To the Shores of Tripoli

Wererat

Darwin's Quest: The Search for the Ultimate Survivor

Assorted Short Stories

Venus: A Paleolithic Short Story
Secession
Duty
Semper Fidelis

Non-Fiction

Exercise for a Longer Life

Author Website
http://www.jonathanbrazee.com